Philip Gee was born in Du[...] most of his life in South A[...]

He now lives in London a[...] Surveyor.

A Soutie Goes Home is his debut novel.

PHILIP GEE

A SOUTIE GOES HOME

+ POSITIVE
PUBLISHING

A Positive paperback

First published in Great Britain by Positive Publishing in 2007

A catalogue record for this book is available from the British library.

Printed and bound in Great Britain.

Acknowledgements

Special thanks to Sally Robertson and Roy Maber.

To Frank,

I hope you enjoy my little book, described as a novel but it is all true

Regards

Philip

—

For Liz, a great human being.

RICHARD MARTYN WESTCOTT (1792-1877)

Chapter One

Tamerton Foliott

In May one thousand seven hundred and ninety two, I came into this world. I happened to learn this by looking into an old family bible. This event happened in a small village in the county of Devon, named Tamerton Foliott, about five miles from Plymouth. The village is pleasantly situated on a branch of the Tamar between hills of no great elevation, of a rather barren and rocky soil. The sides of the hills are often covered with furze and coppice wood, and the subsoil is generally primitive rock, a sort of bastard slate schist, or what the Germans call Grauwacken. The hills are therefore poor, but the valleys are fertile meadows and orchards. A clear rivulet generally runs through, in which small trout are almost always found, and eels.

This village appears to have possessed some notoriety in former times according to a work published about thirty years ago written by a Mrs Grey of Tavistock, titled Warleigh, the Seat of the ancient family of Radcliffe. Warleigh is a very old mansion situated at the mouth of the Tavey, a branch from the Tamar, rather noted in olden times as a fine salmon stream. About five miles up this river is a modern handsome mansion, built by Sir Manesse Lopez, formerly an Israelite, who it is said changed his religion and professed Christianity, for the purpose of acquiring an estate, which he did by purchasing the manor of Maristowe, and also of Beer Alston and Beer Jervis, which contains mines, and is famous for its cherry gardens. These parishes, before the Reform Bill, sent two Members to Parliament, who were of course the nominees of Sir Manasse Lopez. The river Tavey which is acrossed by ford above Maristowe on horseback, and by foot- passengers in a boat, now proceeds upwards through a deep wooded dell (the rocks have here been worked for minerals but without success), goes on towards Buckland Monochoram. On its banks is a castle or abbey, once the property of Sir Francis Drake, the great circumnavigator, in which is an oak table formed of the ship in which he circumnavigated the world. A branch of the Tavey now crosses the Roborough Down at a place called Horrabridge; another runs to Tavistock, Dartmore lying on its east. Some valuable mines are about here, and afar is the railway station.

Of course after the elaborate description of the country, you will expect the production of an extraordinary character, but will be disappointed in that it is only the struggles of a poor lad to fight his way through the world against difficulties and without friends.

My father in those days, was considered a respectable tradesman, a manufacturer of woollen goods, homely but strong and durable, when the wedding dress of a farmer's wife descended as an heirloom for generations, which was crowned by a scarlet cloak by which our matrons of the last century, appeared on the heights near Plymouth, frightened away the army of Bonaparte appearing off Plymouth for the invasion of England.

My father must have been, when a young man, quite a beau. I recollect having seen his wedding coat, which was bright orange, with guilt buttons; of course, in compliment to the Prince of Orange, which shows he was a staunch protestant and Tory, and no Jacobite. His shirt was fine Holland, brought in those days from that watery country, and I am told, with cambric frills, cost about one guinea; small clothes or breeches with knee buckles; silk stockings with silver buckles in his shoes. The aforesaid description is the wedding dress of my worthy Pater. I can testify, as years after, when a grown lanky youth, this very coat was dyed some sober colour and made up for self with a pair of doeskin breeches, which being indestructible, had lasted up to this time. But I must go back again thirty years. About 1760, when this display of finery took place, which, as it happened about thirty years before I was born, I cannot give you any description of, neither can I describe the lady or her dress, as all remains of that had disappeared, utilised undoubtedly by the second wife, who, unfortunately for my father, took her place. The first marriage then evidently took place under auspicious circumstances, but unfortunately I have no data to give as to who she was, her name, family, when she was born, or where they were married. I think it likely I may have heard all these particulars. I am very certain she was a worthy, exemplary woman, because he was always regretting her. She bore him six children, three boys and three girls; two of the latter were delicate, pretty woman, so I calculate was their mother. I understand she died in childbed, and I believe her husband left the neighbourhood in consequence. However, when I was born, he was living in Tamerton, in a large roomy building, which evidently had been an inn, and it was called Cann House Tenement. It had a stone porch over the door; it had large offices behind; a malthouse, brewhouse, and large cellars. There were besides a barn and stables at the back, an orchard about 4 acres; at the bottom a millstream and pond; which was a reservoir for storing water. There were meadows containing about 20 acres of pastureland. At the bottom of all, the rivulet as clear as crystal, as all the brooks in Devon are. Cann House was the first in the village from Plymouth, and opposite was a pretty cottage almost covered with Virginian creeper. Above and below was a high stonewall, enclosing gardens. Between this wall and the road was left a space of waste grassland on which every August was held a fair. This cottage, gardens, orchards and meadows which extended along the road to Plymouth belonged to a Mr. Grigg, a tea merchant of Plymouth, it is said a distant relation. Nearly in front of Cann House was the village green and church, which divides the two roads leading to the village. On this green in August every year was held the fair; the first day for cattle, the second for amusements, in cudgel playing or single stick, and afterwards wrestling. At the southern angle of this green is still the famous old oak tree, many hundreds of years, some say, old. It was flourishing, when I was a boy, and under it when a very little fellow I have sat for many hours at a time, reading some little book, for which I had a passion from the very earliest time I have any recollection of, which made my poor old father very proud, and I often heard him tell his friends he meant to make me a parson. And it is very strange the same feeling descended to his second son Peter, my brother, who had three sons; the second of them was precocious in learning, but has not fulfilled his father's wish by taking Orders.

I must now go back to the year 1790, when my father was a widower with six children. This compelled him, I suppose, to take another wife, for two reasons, first to take care of his young family, second to take care of his business; and here it is necessary to go back a hundred years, and to describe the state of society in the last century. It may be a matter of opinion whether it was happier than the present, or whether the sum total of human happiness and virtue has gained or lost by the wonderful discoveries in Arts, Science, Mechanics, Chemistry, Astronomy, and every other branch of knowledge, Printing, Engraving, and all mankind was supposed to have been promised by selling himself to the Devil.

I have again run away and must go back. My father, I have I think told you, was a manufacturer of woollen goods. He first bought the wool of the farmer; he then sorted it, washed it, carded it, and brought it into a fit state for spinning. This was effected by taking it in packs on horseback round the country for miles, and leaving a portion at every cottage, and collecting the worsted or thread; at the same time in these excursions he also took with him samples of manufactured goods for sale. The spun wool on being brought home had to undergo other processes; some of the worsted had to be steeped in size made with glue. This formed the chain or warp to be passed through the loom and formed into cloth.

I have been particular in describing the divided process in manufacturing the common articles of wearing apparel which 100 years ago constituted the common and universal clothing of mankind, not only the living, but the law compelled you to have the shrouds for the dead made of flannel, under a penalty.

When I say that woollen was the universal article of clothing, we must reflect that cotton was not known before the United States of America was peopled. Wool, silk, flax and skins were the only materials used for clothing, and leather. But in all these materials we know as silk, wool, linen, and some other vegetable substances, considerable skill had been acquired, but many other manufactories were carried on in the same small way in country villages, tan pits, flax pits. And now burst on the world the advent of mechanical power, Spinning Jennies that would spin hundreds of threads at once, shut up the interesting little machine, the spinning wheel, which when I was a boy, filled every cottage. Soon followed the power loom for manufacturing the cloth, and every other part of human labour was beaten down by machinery, and men were only wanted for slaughtering one another.

This revolution extended through almost every mechanical art; manual power was dispensed with, and even horsepower was superseded. Rapidity and cheapness was now the magnum bonam of earthly desires, and yet after having lived eighty years in the world, we are gotten old just the same, and what have we done, what have we done more than we did eighty years ago in the old humdrum way?

To return to 1792, my father took to himself another wife, of course some years younger than himself, and soon began investing in that unprofitable manufacture - a second family. And here began my own personal history, of which my memory is from an early age. I recollect some very unusual bustle in the house; my "mother" was not visible, and old Jack was saddled and with a pillion behind – evidently a seat for a female. From the journey occupying several hours, it was evidently some distance to fetch this Femme Sage, or Sage Femme, and there was some mystery about this. Later on in my life it became clear that she was my fathers' mistress and I and my brother Peter were born to her but I do not have a clear recollection of being introduced to the young stranger. And although it appears that a visitor of the same sort appeared every year about the time of the cuckoo, it did not appear to cause any surprise. The principle recollection besides at this time were some apple trees behind the house, under one of which I used to sit in the summer mornings reading a small book, which no doubt I had as a gift. The old oak on the village green which I believe still exists, was another favourite study under which I sat in the summer time. The village fair, held in August, also brings recollections of sweetmeats and large quantities of cherries; numbers of horses also were stabled on the premises. I recollect also a Quaker's Meeting held in our barn, in which a female addressed the meeting on religious subjects. Up to this time everything appears to have gone on prosperously. At this time I think I had left the old lady who taught us the first rudiments of learning, could read the Prayer Book, Testament, etc., and learnt the Collect for the day every Sunday, and was therefore a pupil in the village school, the master of which bore the name of Smith, and had been a hairdresser at Tavistock, and notwithstanding was well qualified to teach reading, writing and arithmetic, and some of whose sons made a name in the world.

Chapter Two

The Diet of the Poor

And now begin our first troubles. As I have said before, the introduction of machinery was beginning to interfere with all manufacturing trades, and agriculture also. I recollect there were riots and burnings, partly from the dearness of food, but also the introduction of threshing and other machines; but it was not until the present century was fairly established that the effect of woollen manufacturing was really felt, for the great durability of the old manufacturing held its ground for years after. But now came the Conqueror Pride; the new manufactured articles were so superior in appearance and cheapness, the old hand looms were obliged to give way.

Besides the woollen trade, my father rented a small farm of twenty acres and grass and orchard land, chiefly on account of a fine stream of water which ran through the bottom of it, and which was necessary for cleansing the wool and bleaching it, and for keeping a horse and some cows. The orchard often grew cider enough to pay the rents – all useful in bringing up a family of young children.

We are now arrived at the latter end of the last century, and the beginning of our misfortunes and troubles. In the village there lived the family of a lawyer, Mr. Elford, one of the most respectable in the county, whose place of business was Plymouth, but his country house was here. I have a recollection that they were a kind and charitable people, and looked up to and respected, as people of that class usually were in those days, as Radicalism and Communism had not made its way into the villages. In those days, unfortunately, Squire Elford, as he was usually called, was possessed of a small estate on the other side of the brook, so that the small property my father rented was a desirable acquisition to the lawyer's estate. He therefore purchased it for what would now be considered a mere trifle. This of course would be considered by the present unsentimental world, a perfectly legal transaction, which of course it was; but to my father it was a deathblow, as the premises with the stream of water were so particularly suited for the business, and such as could not be easily found. The lawyer, however, did not see the hardship or cruelty, as it really was in this case, as similar could not be obtained in the neighbourhood. A notice to quit was served, and now it seemed that the notion of tenant-right prevailed even in England, and that as long as a man paid rent, it was cruel and unjust, if not illegal, to turn him out. But there is no sentimentality in law, and the notice to quit not being attended to, an ejectment followed, with a beautiful series of legal processes ending in arrest and lodgement in jail.

And now comes my first trial and feeling of disaster, which I feel even now. I suppose I may have been between four and five years of age – a little fellow. Trouble and lamentation was in the house. I recollect it was a fine morning, but the pools in the road were lightly frozen, and icicles were hanging from the eaves of the house, when some men came and took my father away to jail. This I must say arose from his perverse obstinacy, as he could have paid and had friends who would have paid, and ultimately did pay, the costs (yet like the celebrated O'Connell was determined to die on the floor of the house). But in spite of himself he was liberated a poorer, if not a wiser, man. After some difficulty he found what had been a farmhouse in a glen by the side of the brook. This very old and dilapidated building, we occupied the next winter, which was one of great severity. The frost was so severe that the flocks of starlings, thrushes, etc., were so tame they might have been taken by hundreds. And here we little ones, I do not know how many, were all laid up with measles, whooping cough, and scarlet fever. Times were bad, there was almost famine in the land; black bread, a few peas, a little rice, a red or salt herring, a little oatmeal and milk, was the diet of the poor. But God tempers the North wind to the shorn lamb; we children all recovered, my father took a house in the village, the times were better, the first family of six were all out in the world, and were doing well, all except the youngest William, who understood the business, and stuck to his father and helped us. We attended the grammar school of Mr. Smith and soon acquired all the knowledge he could teach us. And now the difficulty was what to do with us. We were not very strongly built, and were not very fit for hard work. One day my father came home from Plymouth, and I was assisting in some farming operations, and told me he had got a situation in the shop of an apothecary and druggist, to which accordingly I was apprenticed for seven years. Here of course I was employed in pounding pills and making plasters, and however it may be despised, the knowledge of pharmacy I acquired, I find very useful even now.

And here I must go back again a few years to describe events, which mark the time. I was present at Davenport soon after the battle of Trafalgar and the death of Nelson, and saw the disabled ship, the Victory, in which Nelson was killed. Seven years before, my uncle George was one of the celebrated "band of brothers" who served in Nelson's fleet and he was the only commander to be killed in the battle of the Nile in Aboukir bay. George, my father's eldest brother joined the navy when just a lad when the family were baker's in Honiton. This family was not well known to us but I remember my father's grief on hearing of his death. George was the commander of the Majestic and on following the Bellerophon ran her jib boom into the main rigging of the Hereux and the Tonnant and was fired into by both ships. George was about the first that fell shot by a musket ball through the throat. When Nelson was on his way to join the Channel Fleet under Lord St Vincent in January, 1801 he requested that Captain Westcott's mother should be presented to him and on hearing that she had not received her son's medal, removed the gold one he was wearing and gave it to her saying "he hoped it was of no less value because he had worn it."

A few years later I was on Roborough Down on which a camp of 30,000 men was formed, who afterwards embarked for Portugal under Sir John Moore, a fine set of men in perfect condition. And a few years later, when settled in Plymouth, I witnessed the return of the survivors after their defeat at the Battle of Corunna, with their wives and children, and a poor, ragged, starved set they were. But the people of Plymouth clothed and fed them; *but they were the first example of the effect of glorious war.* Because of my uncle's record in the Navy, I was offered a birth in a ship, but had no stomach for fighting.

But now to return to the shop, my master Mr. Rendall, was a handsome, gentlemanly person; he wore powder, and was dressed by a professional every morning. He was rather above forty years. He had married a lady, the sister of the Rev. Mr. Spry, Vicar of Crediton. She was handsome, but rather deformed; was a most amiable, religious person, a great believer in the celebrated Calvinistic preacher, Dr. Hawker, for whose person I felt a great reverence, and who then, as I do now, I believed to be the most perfect representative of the great Apostle, St. Paul, but whose preaching I cannot say made the same impression upon me as it did on the female part of the congregation of the New Church. But I preferred the quiet doctrine of Dr. Gandy at the old Church of St Andrew, and I once heard the sermon of an Unitarian minister, and was much struck with the argumentative eloquence, but had sense enough even then to see that the doctrine was unsound and dangerous. And here I must diverge again to say a word in favour of the old system of Bible teaching, as about this time Dissenting Chapels were extending in the villages. Baptists and Methodists were the chief sects. Undoubtedly the Bible, the Old and New Testaments are the authorities on which our belief in the doctrines of Christian religion are founded; and well will they stand the test of examination, that is if we enter into it with that sober spirit of examination. And first begin by examining ourselves and acknowledging our own imperfections; and here arises the danger and difficulty of the study, and the impossibility of our minds comprehending the wonderful attributes of the Deity, incomprehensible, eternal, immortal, and everlasting. 'Tis true, there are talented men who do not believe in the existence of anything but matter and its attributes, heat, cold, electricity, attraction, magnetism; but these are all the qualities of matter only, and they do of themselves account for combination, changes, transformations on the surface of our Globe, and all of the other Globes in endless number, visible and invisible, where there is no beginning and no end, where all is eternity. But here the qualities and actions of matter can be seen and understood. Here we stop. Now we ask what is life, what is this that is added to living matter, or rather causing matter to live? Then the next question is, Mind. This is a quality of living matter possessed in every diversity of degree, even by man himself, from the highest degree of human intellect, to the lowest insect, which we tread upon. These religious ideas were those that I had imbibed about this time, when at the age of about 15 years, and they have not varied much up to this time. But while I admit that the Bible is the true fount from which we draw the true principles of the Christian religion, I cannot admit that every weak-minded enthusiast is a proper expounder of the mysteries therein contained.

the famous old oak tree, many hundreds of years, some say, old.

Chapter Three

Apprenticeship

And now here properly begins the history of my life. My master was a druggist and apothecary, and also sold tea, sugar, oils and colours. All these matters I soon mastered, and having brought with me a small sum I had saved in the country, I made the first investment by going to Haydon's the bookseller, and ordering a new addition of the Pharmacopaea, I believe about 8/- or 9/-, about 1808 or 1809. This having fallen into the hands of my master after I had been studying it a year or two, as the book was in Latin my master did not understand a word of it, and in fact had not seen it, and was perfectly astonished to see such a book in my hands. From this time my master was suspicious and jealous and did everything he could to keep me down, as he certainly had no idea of making me a professional man or a gentleman. But as I was an apprentice for seven years to make myself useful, he endeavoured to do this by employing me in all sorts of occupations-pharmacy, pounding and powdering drugs, making ointments, plasters, pills, tinctures, spirits.

Being clever at and having a taste for painting, I was employed in painting all sorts of fancy articles; but one day his jealousy was roused. A respectable young man came in and requested to see me; and I believe in most towns the druggist's assistants are consulted by a certain class of patients, and also for children. All these things excited the distrust of my worthy master, that he was advised to place a steady and pious young man to watch-in fact, as a spy. This I could not bear; but as indentures of apprenticeship were in those days serious things, and you were liable to imprisonment for any infringement. However, I determined to leave, and having packed up in a bundle all my household goods, and having about 25/- in my pocket, I started one fine morning in June.

I took the road to Tavistock, and crossed over to Dartmoor prison, which was then occupied by French prisoners. I travelled about fourteen miles, and at a beer-shop had a glass of beer and bread and cheese. It now became very hot, and all my worldly goods, although small in quantity and smaller in value, were still a sad burden to carry. However I travelled on to Moreton Hamstead, a small village in which the French officers whose friends were able to support them, were allowed to reside, and a certain degree of liberty around the place being allowed them. And I have heard that a certain tinge of French blood is still observed in the inhabitants. The next day I had a short walk to Exerter, where I obtained a poor lodging. On the third day of my travels I took a walk on the Northernhay. Here I met a man, who observing I was an idler, asked me if I wanted a job. I said I did. He said what trade. I told him I was a middling painter. He said, can you paint the cabins of a ship? Yes. Then come down to Topsham to-morrow morning to Mr. -----. He is building a West Indiaman and will employ you. Accordingly next morning I started for this pretty little seaport, and found they were building a sloop for the West Indian trade, which we finished in a month. I had the gratification of being launched in her, and was taken to Exmouth, where I received above four pounds for wages. And my kind mistress was deputed to settle, and not being very clever at figures, and one pound notes being in circulation, my worthy hostess in mistake paid me a five pound one instead of one. This I did not discover until I had gone some miles on my road to Exerter, and on calculating the amount in my purse. I at once started back to Topsham. The old lady was not pleased with her mistake, and did scarcely thank me for my trouble. When I got to Exerter, I bought a few things, fit for London, and on the Saturday I took my passage in Russell's Wagon for London. This operation took a whole week. Among the passengers was a married woman and child from Plymton near Plymouth. Here of course I should soon have been known had I told my true story. I therefore gave my mother's name – Martyn. I did not find travelling by wagon at all disagreeable, although it took me a week. Being young, I took the opportunity of walking by day, and had therefore the chance of seeing the whole country, and shall never forget the sensation of the first view of Salisbury spire on coming over the Downs from Dorchester. Our manner of living was very frugal – a cup of milk and bread for breakfast – a cup of beer, bread and cheese for dinner. And so we travelled on. On nearing London my female friend appeared anxious about my safety, and on enquiring what money I had, persuaded me to let her have a sovereign to take care of. And being quite a stranger and friendly I did so, and in this I was right, as I, as the lawyers say, thereby got a locus standi. This woman was a decent, nice-looking woman, and I was placed in a bedroom adjoining, I soon found out that the husband had imbibed a degree of jealousy about his wife's travelling companion. The lady, I believe, soon satisfied her husband that I was quite an innocent youth, and my trusting her with a sovereign convinced him of the truth. In fact we were all right. Although ready enough to fall in love with a damsel of the right sort, yet a married woman with children such a thing never entered my mind, and to this innocence and simplicity I attribute my safety, and that living in London from 17 to 24, I never fell into vices and the indulgences young men often do, God knows. My simple prayer:- Preserve me during the night from all harm;direct me to that which is good. Alone in London without friends, without means, there was always a something near me, which seemed to support and bear me up. And although others may doubt and ridicule the idea of a superintending Providence, I am perfectly convinced that all the chief events of my life have not been dependent on my own will.

"There is a Providence which shapes our ends, Mishew them as we will."

I must now return to my old master at Plymouth. Whether my dropping my name of Westcott and adopting that of Martyn, my mother's name, prevented the discovery of who I was, I cannot tell. I was never put to trouble or inconvenience. Perhaps my old master never took the trouble to make enquiries. However, it is clear it would be much more difficult to remain in cog.now. My master, however, had a better opinion of me the first year or two, as he was desirous of obtaining my brother's services for a nephew of his, a Mr. Spry, a son of the Rev. Mr. Spry, Vicar of Credition, whom he had settled at St. Thomas' Exeter as a druggist. And here it may seem strange with what facility we both acquired the knowledge of drugs and business in general; and compare it to the want of success in those young gentlemen, who although supported by wealthy friends, by superior position in society, and superior education, went down in the scale of society, while we with all the disadvantages of poverty, and the world's opinion against us, have succeeded in establishing a position from which they have fallen, and oftentimes have dragged their families with them. Perhaps you will say – why change your name, as you had done nothing wrong? I had been apprenticed for seven years, and to leave without consent of the master you were liable to imprisonment, and might perhaps have been sent on board a ship of war, as men in those days were scarce, and government was not particular how it got them.

However, here I am now in London in a poor lodging in Colman Street, Cheapside, lodging at the house of a shoemaker, who and his wife too happened to be natives of Plymton near Plymouth. This gave us a sort of tie of countrymanship, and I felt a sort of homeness in this poor man's house. It was a very strange feeling to awake in this strange city sixty years ago, listening all night to the striking and chimes of twenty or thirty clocks, the cry of the old watchmen as they were called; although the noise by night and the traffic by day was not one twentieth part what it is now here, in 1810 or 1811. I was a lad of 17 without friends, without money, without a character, trade or profession; while I left my brother Peter at Exeter, very smugly off with Mr. Spry, who I am afraid was employing himself not very profitably, as a few years afterwards I heard his business had failed and my brother had gotten another situation in Bristol, with a Mr.Hartwell, who also failed in business. But notwithstanding, Peter had prospered, and being a handsome lad, was a general favourite.

I must now return to my own troubles; as the little money I had was slowly melting away, I became anxious to find the means of earning something. On strolling about Whitechapel and the Commercial Road, I met a man who addressed me: "Shipmate, do you want a job?" I answered, I did. He said he was working at the East India dock, getting a ship ready for the East Indies. He would get me some employment. We accordingly started, and on arriving there I was at once employed painting the cabin. The job lasted about four weeks, during which time I had to walk back to London every night. And during the whole of that time the beautiful and wonderful comet was hanging overhead. Had this any connection with those terrible events, which were occurring, and did occur for the next few years? After the ship was finished I got employment with a housepainter in the borough; being employed to paint the windows of a house four stories high, I had to sit outside on a board, a most dangerous position. I gave it up. And going into the Royal Exchange I saw on the wall a number of advertisements. One was: - Wanted, a young man who could write well and keep accounts and attend to the business of an outfitter, that is a person who supplies shipping with everything. This place was in Ratcliff Highway. I applied for it. The difficulty was a character for honesty. I gave him my history as far back as Topsham, where I painted a West Indiaman, and returned the five-pound note paid to me in mistake. This was satisfactory; so you see honesty is the best policy. I found Mr. Maxwell was an Irishman, carrying on business as an outfitter, and did business chiefly with Swedes, Norwegians, etc., with whom I was to converse and endeavour to effect sales, but of whose language of course I understand not one word. But in case of difficulty I had to call the wife, a little delicate Irishwoman, but a kind, amiable little body. Another Irishwoman was maid of all work who lived in the kitchen, while the mistress lived upstairs at the back of the shop. Sat on his board was a respectable old man working as a tailor named Dawe. This person was a native of Somerset. Mr. Maxwell appeared to be about 30 years of age, and as far as I could see attended very little to business, and was absent every evening in some of the numerous tea gardens, which abounded in the neighbourhood of London. His favourite amusement was Trap Ball. Here I passed a very quiet life. Of Mrs. Maxwell I saw very little, of her husband rather less. Old Dawe the tailor and Kitty the Irish maid were my chief companions, and very kind and friendly they were. Mrs. M. being almost always left alone, I fear consoled herself with a drop of whiskey. Irish Kitty related to me the horrors of the Irish rebellion in which her family suffered. During this time I lived in Radcliff an explosion of a gunpowder mill occurred, I believe at Hounslow, 30 miles away. And also the most extraordinary thunderstorm occurred, the flashes of lightning were incessant, and the shocks also; the air was filled with the suffocating fumes of sulphur, but I do not recollect of any serious damage being done. While living in this neighbourhood, the horrible murder of the Marrs family occurred, and after that the Williamson, by the same wretched man, who after being taken into custody, hanged himself. I believe the man was insane; the jury's verdict was Felo de se. I saw the body exposed on a hurdle, naked, and afterwards a hole dug in a crossway, the body thrown in and a stake driven through it. This was at a time when a woman was burned for poisoning her husband, when people were hanged for forgery, coining, horse and sheep stealing, shoplifting and many other minor offences. This was at a time when war was destroying 1000 human beings a day, and a philosopher publishing a work endeavouring to pass a law to prevent the increase of population. Here I passed a year or more, and I am afraid Mr. Maxwell did not find his amusement in Trap Ball profitable, as his affairs were obliged to be wound up. I was now anxtious to get back to my first employment, the drug business, and hearing of a gentleman in the Strand, Mr. Midgley, a very respectable Chemist, wanting a person in the laboratory, I applied, and was engaged at a guinea a week. I took lodging with a poor, kind, respectable old lady, a Welsh woman. Here I was employed in making and mixing all the preparations of the old Pharmacopaeia. Distilling Rose water from a glass crucible in a sand bath, or oil of box or oil of bricks from an iron crucible. These were obtained from the decomposition of the fixed oil. Sometimes when Mr. Midgley was away, I made the acquaintance of Mr. Gobb in the shop, and assisted him dispensing, in putting up and packing large quantities of drugs, which we sent in new rum puncheons to the West Indies. To my knowledge, dexterity and cleverness in these matters, I found no difficulty in advancing another step. However, while here, I had a letter from Peter, stating that his master, Mr. Hartwell, had failed, and that was advised to come to London, and if I could assist him. I directed him to my lodgings in the Strand accordingly. In a few days up he came, and as the coach stopped in Piccadilly he had to carry his luggage with a heavy greatcoat. A man who offered to take it for him he discarded, believing all Londoners were thieves, and priding himself on his knowledge and cleverness in not allowing himself to be taken in which he well might have been, having come from Bristol. On observing the poverty of my lodging, he was much cut up; but on my showing him a few yellow boys worth 25/- each, he was better satisfied; for Peter was always a natty young man and carried most of his property externally, while I was always a plain, poor fellow, but liked to have a sound foundation – that is, a few guineas in the pocket.

My brother was better off than myself, as he had some references to druggists in London from Mr. Hartwell, who recommended him to a situation as assistant to a very respectable surgeon in the Strand, which happened to be next door to my place of business, Midgley's. This was another awkward affair, as our positions were different, we could not be known to each other without making known many things which might have lost both our situations. Here we were in that very severe winter which set in on Christmas Eve, and lasted until April, with a thick, heavy fog, and the Thames was frozen over, on which I walked from Blackfriars to London Bridge, and during which the French army was retreating from Moscow.

And now in the spring another misfortune happened. My brother who was living in the house of his master – I forget his name – was taken ill of Typhoid Fever, and I could not see him, although I heard from Midgley's assistant, Mr. Gobb, who was a regular good fellow. However he recovered and got a situation at Henley-on-Thames. And now one of his old Bristol master's sons wrote to him to get him a place. See how things turn about however. Clark Hartwell came up and also the older brother came up and lived in London some years; and I am sorry I cannot give a very good account of them. I know they took a shop in Borough Road, furnished it on credit, and failed, paying sixpence in the pound.

My friend Mr. Gobb, seeing my capabilities, recommended me get a situation as assistant. Accordingly I got a situation with old Mr.Agar in Whitechapel, whose son Frederick had had just left the hospital and was taking his father's business. Another son, Dr. Agar, was giving lectures with Dr. Hooper on medicine. Another son was in practice at Peckham. My predecessor here was the afterwards famous Mr. John Probert, the founder of the Medical College. Here I began to bleed and draw teeth, and dress the broken heads of the Irish men and women, which happened every Saturday night; and here also having plenty of spare time, I began studying medicine and every book I could. Hooper's Vade Mecum, Chemistry, Surgery and Medicine and Anatomy I got by heart. I subscribed to the Minerva Library in Leaden Hall Street-one guinea a year-and read all the books I could get. But authors in those days were scarce. Here also I had the opportunity of seeing all the great men of the day – Ramsbottom, a fine handsome man, London Hospital; Sir William Benjamin, the great Lithotomist of the day; Dr. Babington of the City; little Dr. Lettsom the Quaker, whose motto was: -

When called upon the sick to heal,
I physick, bleed, and sweats 'em.
If after that they choose to die
Why then they must, I Lettsom."

Poor old Mr. Agar and his son Frederick I received the greatest kindness from, and strange to say I was succeeded here by a Mr. Martin, who afterwards took Mr. Westcott's place at Oundle.

Now after being in London several years, Peter and I agreed to go down to the West once more. They were old and poor, and hitherto we had not been able to help them. The girls, of which there were five, were some married, all supporting themselves and helping their father and mother, and living with William who was still carrying on the business.

On returning to London, I had to get another situation with Mr. Hill, Cooper's Row, Tower Hill. He was a fine, handsome man, kept his horse and gig, and had a fair partner. We did not agree very long, so I left and took lodgings in the Borough in Tooley Street. Here, seeing the name of Smith on a grocer's shop, I entered and found a son of my old schoolmaster, who was married to the daughter of an undertaker. Here I attended some lectures of Sir Astley Cooper, also some lectures on Mechanics by Allen of Plough Court. Here I obtained a situation with Saumerez and Dickson. These gentlemen had a very large practice at Newington Butts, and in the Surgery kept two assistants. My partner was Mr. Perry, the son of a medical man at Deddington. Perry was a good fellow, rather slow, was enamoured of a farmer's daughter, who a few months later he married, and I believed turned farmer and bred a large stock of boys and girls. I never saw him after. On his leaving, Mr. Dickson asked me if I could undertake the whole of the dispensing, which amounted to about 100 patients a day. Now let it be understood that out of 100 patients on the books, about 80 of them had repetitions of the same medicine, repeated for many days following; say perhaps 30 of them had saline draughts or mixtures, 20 perhaps had tonic or infusion of Colomb, so that after a few days I had them all arranged in my own mind and could put them up with great facility, without reference to the prescriptions; and if asked could tell from memory what 19 out of 20 of the patients were taking. Such was the effect of practice on a memory so retentive that I could tell exactly what each of the partners had been giving his patient when he himself had entirely forgotten. For nearly two years I worked from seven in the morning until ten at night every day in the week, Sundays not excepted; when I began to feel the want of a little relaxation, and accordingly took a situation at Brighton with an old gentleman by the name of Dix- a kind old gentleman and sister, one of the very old school, but whose practice was largely in midwifery, and when I studied such works as Denman and had plenty of practice too among the lower classes. And I recollect that the first patient that I attended was on the very night the Princess Charlotte died. Here I had plenty of time for study, and here I read every medical work I could get, and they were by no means numerous in those days. But what was Brighton at that time? It contained about six medical men. Hall, Bond and Brewster, a firm, there was one in Ship Street and a Mr. Badcock. A few came down with the Prince Regent who was building the Pavilion at that time. Perhaps Brighton at that time contained about 5000 inhabitants. My brother who had been living with Mr. Walker of St. John Street, and was apothecary to the Prince Regent at Carlton House, had been attending lectures on Medicine, went up to the Apothecaries Hall and passed.

Having saved from my salary about £80 I went to London

and paid the necessary fees for the lectures necessary to pass the Apothecaries Hall. I set to work attending two lectures daily on Anatomy and dissection, at Brookes Brands Chemistry, Pearson of St. George's and others, and in less than six months went up to the hall and passed. It is true; I had been studying six years while an assistant, and had obtained considerable practice and knowledge. So that we both of us had got on thus far without help, but had to assist the poor old folks at home by sending them £10 yearly. I on my part rather gloried in having beaten poverty and the world, and boasted of it, and followed Burns' advice to his son, and

"To gather gold on every hand
 That justified by honour
 Not for to hide it in a hedge,
 Nor for a train attendant,
 But for the glorious privilege
 Of being independent."

The Fatal Oak, Tamerton

The Fatal Oak

This postcard view of the large old oak tree is thought to have been taken during the 1880s and shows Cann Cottages in the background. Both tree and cottages are still part of the village scene and long may they be so.

Chapter Four

Martock

Now my brother Peter and I both prospered working in London, but after a time, and being many years in a humdrum place, moved to the village of Martock in Somerset. Although I had never felt the need to marry, Peter had a wife and a brood of six one of which was named William Wynn whom was very precocious in learning and whom later I adopted after Peter had passed away in 1858. William excelled in all aspects of his life and in medicine and went on to become a Coroner of London and also the author of many medical books and journals. From a very early time in William's life it was clear that he possessed an exceptional ability and we became close friends from that time and on all through his life to this time as he has continued with the practice here in Martock as I have now grown old.

Although this world of ours for several centuries had been undergoing wonderful transformations and changes from 1600 to the present time, beginning with the American War, the French Revolution in 1790 to the present time; now all these changes arise and have arisen from the actions and passions of men, for Nature and the laws which govern the Universe are I believe the same as they were some thousands of years ago. The sun from my bedroom window rises and peeps over the same spot on Ham Hill to a minute as it did 40 years ago, and if there is a difference in time, the fault is not in the sun, but in the measure of time. Of all living matter man alone is erratic and changing; all creation else is governed by Nature's laws which are made for them and do not change, except so far as they are changed by man himself. And in that respect, the power of man is limited; But mankind does endure and now the new worlds are opening up with Australia and Africa being colonised by British and European settlers and wonderful stories filtering back home of great progress and triumphs against difficult odds. My half sister Anne who is a bright and pretty young woman had married a gentleman of some means a Robert Polyblank of Plymouth. Soon after a daughter was born to them and she was named Mary Grace, and I did visit there once when I was in Plymouth. I found Polyblank to be a most amiable fellow but a man who seemed unhappy with the state of things in England and was enamoured of the idea of the new colonies and even spoke of immigrating to Australia. My poor sister could not dissuade her worthy husband and so in the early part of 1830 they boarded a ship bound for the new world in Australia. We understood from their letters that the journey had been particularly stormy and with my sister and her young daughter suffering considerable discomfort and sea sickness. Cape Town was it seemed a welcome relief for the weary traveller's and after seeing the unbridled beauty of their surroundings and the orderliness of the streets and houses in the town they decided to travel no further and disembarked there. Many years later and after my niece Mary Grace had married her husband, Steven and all had moved to Natal to grow sugar cane and she set about producing eleven children. And so our family spread to the colonies and later on one of William's, my adopted son's offspring did marry Albert, the last of the eleven children.

photo Richard Major

<u>Note 33</u>   Bridge House - Westcott's Martock home

Chapter Five

SOUTIE

"Hey Soutie, Why don't you go back where you came from man?"

I am not proud to admit that I am able to trace my ancestry in Colonial South Africa through several generations of drunken fornicators. Our time in Africa began with my great grandfather Steven, who arrived in Cape Town South Africa in 1830. It is not clear as to why he left Malaysia but we gather that it was in order to avoid some unpleasantness' there. As luck would have it and at about this time Mr and Mrs Polyblank arrived in Cape Town with their daughter Mary Grace who became Steven's long suffering wife. Steven moved his new wife and her parents to Natal to grow sugar cane and then set about producing eleven children, and one illegitimate one for which he was required to pay damages to her family in the sum of two hundred and fifty pounds. The fallen maiden, was the youngest daughter of a well-known Natal family and had to be hastily married off in order to avoid any further humiliation. We can only surmise as to what society was like at that time, the great trek had begun with land hungry settlers moving north to farm and the battle of blood river still a recent memory. The great Zulu Nation controlled Zululand where Piet Retief and his party had died at the hands of Dingaan. Durban was growing into a modern port with roads and infrastructure taking shape and, churches and schools being built. As people prospered big mansions were built to rival those in England and colonial snobbery took hold and flourished, surviving in many quarters up until this time.

Steven owned and farmed "Saccharine," a sugar farm near Veralum north of Durban that is today Mount Edgecombe. In the early days of sugar farming the farmers crushed their cane on the individual farms and Steven had his own milling equipment that he had imported from overseas. The ship that carried it had sunk in Table Bay but luckily it was salvageable and shipped up to Durban and installed on the farm. He was obviously very proud of it as we had a photograph of it at home and as I recall it looked like a giant ring press with two huge rollers and a giant gear on the end to turn them. Steven also had the singular distinction of being the first sugar farmer to grow sugar on a slope as until this time it was believed to be impossible. Steven I suppose prospered to a degree and had business interests in Durban as well as his farm and was in the habit of riding into town for sorties which no doubt involved heavy drinking and whoring sessions with his reprobate friends and then wandering back to the farm in a drunk and abusive condition. This continued until his eldest daughter grew up and in defence of her mother took a shambok (cow hide whip) to him and gave him a sound thrashing. He was so incensed by the assault on his person that he left the farm never to be seen again. Rumour has it, that he went transport riding carting goods from the Port of Durban to the new Goldfields on the reef. His death was registered in Harrismith in the Orange Free State so I imagine that he lies buried where he fell on the trail some way either side of Harrismith. I like to believe that he is buried in the foothills of the Drakensburg Mountains just below Van Reenen's pass in that beautiful valley that greets you when you drive into Natal from the Highveld.

My grandfather Thomas was much calmer than his father and although he did work for a short time for the Natal Steam Railway he spent most of his life in Gentlemanly pursuits like tennis walking and fishing. Thomas owned an Ox Wagon and team of oxen that he would use to ply up and down the coast between Durban and East London, beach combing, camping and fishing and living off the land. He was a wonderful fisherman with a rod and real and this rubbed off on my uncle Philip who caught some huge fish in his day. Dare I say it but I imagine that a fair amount of family have survived to this day among the coloured population in the area. Thomas lived at Tamerton an old colonial double story in Rapson Road in Durban, since demolished to make way for a block of flats, with his unmarried sisters enjoying an untroubled gentlemanly life until he eventually married my grandmother when he was in his fifties and she was in her early twenties. It came as quite a shock to his sisters when he wandered home from visiting some friends and announced that he was to be married. My father and his brother were their offspring, but the pair was very different in character and never really got on with one another. My uncle Philip was a happy go lucky laid back character while his brother Wynn my dad was very erratic and uptight man. Both of them drank far too much in later life and as teenagers were spoilt rotten by their maiden aunts, whom had left them a small fortune which amount they were to inherit at the age of 21. My late father was the first beneficiary, this event took place after his 21st birthday on 13th May 1934, and he set about spending his windfall with grace and style. He took passage on a ship bound for Southampton and spent some months in England wining and dining the young ladies there. On his return it was not long before he had spent all of his inheritance and had to seek gainful employment. Dad was more English than the English and very proud of his involvement in World War 2. He was captured by Rommel at Tabrouk and spent the rest of the war as a P O W (prisoner of war). As the Allied forces advanced on Germany he took part in the prisoner's forced march for one hundred miles across Germany and into Italy where he was finally freed. Although he was always a slight man he was six feet tall but weighed less than one hundred pounds, about 7 stone, at the end of the war. After being rescued by the Allies he was sent to England to await passage home during which time he met and beguiled my late mother into joining him in Durban where they were married in 1948. My mother had been married before the war to a man called Thacker, but we understand that the marriage had largely broken down before the war started. I remember that Thacker lived in Australia after the war and he died in 1966. My mother was very secretive about her life in England and our feeling was that her young life had not been particularly happy, and when we questioned her about her father, even in later life when we were older, all she would say was that he died. Although we never met Granny May mom's mother she was a big part in our lives as every birthday, and Christmas a card and postal order for 5 shillings and as we got older 10 shillings would arrive. In my memory she never ever forgot, but my mother never returned to England and never saw her mother again before her death in 1969. On a visit to England in 1992 I investigated mom's family at the records office, her maiden name was Pament, and she was born in 1918 so I began looking for her "father's" registration of death. I searched up until 1925 without result. As mom would have been 7 years old by then I began searching backwards and found that he had died of consumption in 1914. I suppose that being illegitimate in those days was quite awkward and difficult. I also found that mom's name at birth had been registered as Compton and so we assume that this was the name of her real father, but later when she was about 16 years old her name was re-registered back to Pament. Granny May was a young woman of 29 years of age, in the prime of her life when this occurred and I like to think that Compton was perhaps killed in the final stages of the first world war, rather than being a bit of a cad, and absconding after the event. Was he even aware that he was going to be a father? Sadly we will never know!

I presume that my parents did enjoy some happiness during their marriage but from my earliest memory there was tension between them and in the house as my grandmother ruled the roost. Mom and Dad were often at each other's throats and when we were very small there were long periods when he was absent from home. My elder sister, my twin sister, and I were the result of the union that at best could only be described as a bit unusual. We were installed in my Grandmother's house as Dad had no money, no prospects and a bit of a drinking problem. Luckily for us my mother was a very hard working and efficient bookkeeper and so we survived the first twenty odd years of our lives. We were burgled one night while he was away and we woke to my mother's screams of terror as she had woken up with the blankets being gently pulled down and a black face looking at her from the bottom of the bed. The burglar ran off but was soon apprehended by the police still in possession of clothing which had my sister's name on a label sewn into the garment. As I recall he was sentenced to six months in jail and six cuts with the heavy cane. There was a positive spin off from the burglary however as after this it was decided that we should get a dog, and Uncle Philip went off to procure one from the SPCA. Sally was duly installed, a shaggy black mongrel who for weeks never uttered a sound but eventually barked at a Zulu woman who had come to the back door. It was a Saturday morning, we were all on the back veranda, Sally was lying under the big old wood table and it was pure simple reaction that caused her to bark. We were all so taken aback but Sally was cheered and petted and after that became a fully integrated part of the family, and she stayed with us for the rest of her long life.

My late mother had strong links to the Roman Catholic Church due to her mum being the cook in a convent where she attended school, and she often spoke of Westminster Cathedral and so when we first visited England we went to mass there. That was in 1992 and since living in London I often visit there for the beauty and peace that one feels inside it's wonderful space and I light a few candles in memory of the departed. Not only is it an Iconic brick building in every sense of the word but is also in my opinion one of the holiest places on earth. It has soaring acoustics that enables perfect sound from the great organ and wonderful choir that sings a Latin mass every single day of the year. The four great brick domes high above that form the roof are, according to one of the priests built that way to allow the souls of the worshipers to soar. It is without doubt one of the most special places in the world and if possible attend a choir or organ recital. Hymns and incantations written 500 years ago by medieval monks all dedicated to God's great glory and all largely forgotten, except here. The Roman Catholic Church had a big influence on my mother's young life and she was our rock later when we were young and growing up.

One night I walked into my parents bedroom after the fighting had become really noisy, my mother was sitting up in bed and sobbing into her hands, dad was standing next to the bed looking quite drunk and clenching and unclenching his fist. I was about fifteen at the time and I looked at them both and said "Please stop fighting?" and I turned and walked out of the room. Dad eventually left when I was eighteen and I didn't see him for ten years, until he pitched up in the town that I was working in like the proverbial bad penny. After an accident when I was tied to the rafters in hospital he did visit me every day for about an hour and we caught up on quite a lot over this period.

It was an interesting time in South Africa with the United Party ousted in 1948 and Afrikaner Nationalism taking over. Dad was opposed to the Nationalists and wrote letters of protests to the newspapers, some of which I found and read much later on. Sadly it was a time when I didn't think much of him and so I threw them away. Dad was a bigot too and he used to refer to our wealthy Lebanese neighbours as "those bloody Arabs". We were forbidden to play with their offspring, which was a major drawback in our young lives, as they possessed the best toys in the neighbourhood. I will never forget the look of hurt on Rodney's face when I told him that my father said that we were not allowed to play with him. He never spoke to me again. When the National Party won the Republic of South Africa vote, Dad was incensed by the upstart Afrikaners to a point where we walked down the hill to Umgeni Road and procured a wooden flag pole from a merchant and carried it all the way home. Gran's bungalow was a typical colonial house with a tin roof and a wide veranda along two sides. The veranda was supported by columns and on arriving home Dad strode up to the corner pillar and stood leaning over the brick balcony and holding up his flag pole at various angles on the corner of the house, the idea being to fly the union jack to display his opposition to the political front and loyalty to Great Britain. Dad being Dad the pole was never erected and lay un-used for some years until us kids used it in a tree house up the avocado pear tree.

One of my earliest memories was of Zulu women who

would knock on the back door with huge baskets of vegetables to trade for old clothes or what have you. My grandmother who lived a very Spartan life would haggle over green mielies, pumpkin or whatever was going in exchange for a bit of material or old clothes. Because these bartering episodes were so one-sided Dad would intercept the women on their way out and slip them some cash in order to even up the deal. Then horror of horrors an Afrikaans family moved in next door, and I was called a "Soutie" for the first time. For those who don't know a "Soutie" is a derogatory term used by some Afrikaners' for English speaking South Africans, someone with one foot in South Africa, one foot in England, with his penis dangling in the salty ocean in between. Time marched on however and in due time I found myself married with wife three children and a mother- in- law thrown in. This particular "Soutie" has grown weary of the tension of living in Africa, the failing economy, and the uncertain future, Comrade Bob up north happily wrecking a great country and being allowed to by the western powers. Combined with the horror of the Congo, Sierra Leone, Angola, and Mozambique all wrecked by tribalism, corruption and greed. Add Ruanda, Ethiopia, the Sudan, Burundi, Somalia, Eritrea and Kenya to the Kaffir Pot (three-legged cast iron pot) and all you get is darkness. Our own rainbow nation of South Africa was supposed to be the guiding light, the ray of hope for Africa to follow. Alas no! South Africa is showing all the signs of being a cock up like the rest. The rainbow nation clearly has no understanding of its new democracy and the murder, mayhem and plunder continues. Along with her neighbours the rainbow nation is busy screwing itself to death. H I V AIDS (which was invented by whites to scare blacks) is totally out of control, but if you get it its not really a problem as the Sangoma (witch doctor) has a cure which usually involves something nasty like sex with a minor or a virgin. Reckless promiscuity by all sections of the populace has fuelled the relentless spread of this invisible killer virus. My old Victorian Grandmother would have said "did you ever what next?"

My old grandmother was something, she lived to be ninety-three and was as tough as teak. She was born in Queenstown, a small 1820 settler village inland from East London and was one of twelve children from two fathers. Her father had died of something or other and I am not sure of the mix of stepbrothers and sisters and full ones. My Grandmother was a very un materialistic old dear who was eligible to claim an old age pension for 28 years of her life but refused to do it as she had never had formal employment and so had never contributed. She was born in 1889 and after a bad illness became a Christen Scientist who boasted that she had not needed a doctor for 40 years, but we grew up under the shadow of their beloved leader Mary Baker Eddie, an American woman that started the cult, and we had a picture of her in the living room. Every Sunday as kids we were dragged off to Sunday school with a bunch of old ladies in hats and taught about mind over matter. The day that I started at boarding school I was told that I no longer had to attend and it was a joyous day and I never went again. My sisters attended for some years after I had stopped. Some of Granny's siblings had died young but the ones that we knew all made old bones. They were very kind to us as children, Aunt Bid & Aunt Meg in particular as they lived in Durban. Aunt Dixie lived in White River so we only saw her once every five or six years. My grandmother's name was Kate and every Wednesday Aunt Bid and Aunt Meg would visit Kate for lovely beans curry and rice. My grandmother god bless her could do a great roast and amazing apple pie but was not renown for her beans curry which consisted of a kind of curry soup with beans in it. Aunt Meg was the crumpet expert and we would look forward to eating them with butter and golden syrup when we came home from school. How I miss those uncomplicated days. Anyway my elder sister Mary came home from school one day and overheard the three old dears ensconced in the drawing room discussing the sputnik and space exploration which was in the news at the time, the conversation went something like this:

"I often wonder if there are other life forms in space" said Biddy

"Oh I'm sure there are" offered Kate "but of course it's much easier for them to come down here than it is for us to go up there."

"Yes of course," agreed Meg and Bid nodding in unison.

They really were from another planet themselves and yet in matters of life they possessed huge intuition and wisdom. I would have liked to know them in maturity.

Another early recollection was the start of a rather un-illustrious school career, and while my sisters sailed effortlessly along, I had a miserable time. Initially I was sent to the Clifton Preparatory High School, in Lambert Road, Durban. Clifton was and still is a very expensive private school for boy's from wealthy and in those day's white only families. My father and his brother were old boys, about the 1920's and after that they attended Durban High School. The problem was that we were not wealthy and survived by living with my grandmother and so when I reached standard one we could no longer afford the fees and I was sent to Durban Preparatory High School, the government prep that in those years cost about two shillings and sixpence a term. The head master at Clifton was Mr Sutcliff, a much respected man, and I think it was

Mrs Wood who looked after the juniors. School for me was a nightmare as I was a bit dyslexic and I think suffered from ADD (Attention Deficit Disorder) and I found learning very difficult. I can still remember a class in which the difference between the and the was being explained and remember feeling a sense of total panic as I had no idea of what they were on about. To this day I don't believe that I could accurately explain the reason for the and the. Anyway in standard two I arrived at Durban Prep and the nightmare continued. Some of my friends were already at prep and so I did know some of the boy's. The headmaster was Tug Wilson who was working out his last day's to retirement and was not overly interested in the place. After "Tug" Mr Gough came to the school, a psychopath by all accounts and I detested the man. He would assemble the school on the tenisette courts and stand above us on the roof of the change rooms, delivering Hitler like speeches, smashing a fist into his other hand to emphasise his point. He had a speech defect, it seemed as if his lips were too big for his mouth and as he barked at us like a gattling gun, spit would fly in all directions. Because of my mental block to learning I fell foul of many teaches who in those days wrote you off as one of the thick ones and I was always in trouble for late homework or doing none at all. The Afrikaans teacher's seemed to be the worst lot as probably due to my father's view's I had no interest in learning their beloved Taal (Language). This led to confrontation, Mevrou Lotter was by far the scariest, she stood about five feet two inches tall and weighed in at about two hundred pounds, all set off with dyed blond hair, and we hated each other. I have lost count of the number of canings that I received during my prep years, often twice in a week, and being sent to the head master twice in a week meant that the flogging metered out on the second visit was far harder than the first. In these modern times I could probably have had them up for assault. Of course it was not all bad and there were some absolute gems among the teachers at that school. Mr Wilkinson the woodwork teacher was one such, who will be remembered fondly by many generations of DPHS pupils who were taught the basics of woodwork in his class. Woodwork was twice a week and it was the highlight of my Prep years. The induction to the woodwork class involved a set of rules on how to behave in the workshop, and what would happen if we broke the rules. Suzy a short piece of South African pine that had Suzy written on it in chalk lived in the cupboard and she we were told would come flying out and beat anyone who transgressed the line. Old Wilky never ever used Suzy because he never had to, he was too well liked. Mrs Demarigny was another wonderful lady who had that special gift as a teacher.

When high school came along it was decided that I should attend boarding school. The financial situation at home although still tight had improved enough so I was enrolled at Kearsney College in Botha's Hill. Although I had failed the entrance exam my father worked for people with strong links to the school and so strings were pulled and I was accepted. The head was Mr Hopkins, a very gentlemanly man but rather old fashioned in thinking who ran the school like a military camp. "Hoppy" I think had been a major during world war two, and the school had strong traditions and links to the glorious past. Every Friday we had cadets and would march around the fields with old rifles that had been decommissioned. In addition our beds had to be made with no creases, hospital corners, and our lockers had to be as neat as a pin. Inspections resulted in beds being stripped and lockers emptied. All good fun it was, but when the army came along it was a bit of a laugh as I had been doing similar things for four years.

My twin sister I believe was the most affected by the instability at home and she never ever forgave my father for the way that he behaved towards the end of his marriage. In the interim she had been dating one Charles Geldard, a very serious quite boring character, who became an electrical engineer but when trying to fix the fridge forgot the basic rule of switching it off before opening the works and he succeeded in blowing it up never to work again. I find that a lot of engineering types are like that, not very practical when it comes to doing technical things. Another ex brother in law was the same, a brilliant chemical engineer but keep him away from anything technical. Once his automatic garage door broke and Katherine my wife had to show him how to repair it. Anyway Charles left my sister I think that they were boring each other to death and my sister in law left her husband, after being used as a punch bag for fourteen years she decided that enough was enough. Katherine and I wasted a lot of time fighting, the first ten years of our marriage was a kind of war of attrition and we had some ding dong battles. I regret those years lost to conflict and would advise any young person contemplating marriage to accurately and concisely list the terms of engagement as it were so that both parties know precisely where they stand. We stuck it out however and eventually if one gives it long enough one settles to a kind of an understanding but bad memories often invade and resentment bubbles to the surface.

" Soutie go home"

Chapter Six

Mapipaan

On the 12th of January 1970, dressed in my one and only ultra conservative charcoal suit I presented myself in the offices of LTA construction Ltd. I had signed a four-year contract with them and in return I would learn the mysteries of modern construction. LTA was formed of the marriage of Lewis Construction of Australia, Thompson Construction of Johannesburg and The Anglo American Corporation. The Durban firm that I joined was largely staffed by Lewis men and it was quite a happy ship. Lewis Construction South Africa was started in 1929 when a young Australian named Blue Schwara who at the age of 29 came to Durban to build the first skyscraper, The Colonial Mutual Building in West Street in Durban. Whether you like it or not the Australians are pretty good at what they do and Lewis Construction grew into a thriving National Company. The managing director of the day was a little Australian called Jim Gregory who was a gentleman of the old school but who ran the company with a rod of iron. Mr Gregory was also known as "Mapipaan" by the native staff because of the pipe that never left his lips and whenever you went in to see him he was obscured behind great clouds of smoke. Whenever you were called up and he said, "spare me a tick" down the line you knew you were in for a rollicking about something or other. Jim was an accountant by trade and incredible good with mental arithmetic. He seldom used a calculator and he personally checked every single invoice that was paid by the company every month. We had a great deal of work on in and around Durban which included the Bay Passage Building, General Accident Building, Durdoc Centre, 320 West Street, John Ross House all modern high rise buildings. My salary was a princely R100.00 per month which amount was to increase every six months by R5.00 per month so that at the end of the contract I was earning R140.00 per month. I used to work really hard and often thought that they may give me a little more but no such luck. Even when I passed my Building Diploma and I took it in to my boss he said "right well make a copy and give it to my secretary to put it on your file." By that stage Jim had retired, as had Jim Reardon a very experienced and solid man and another director Julian Attlee had dropped dead on the floor of the Westville Country Club squash Court. He was a fit 44 but probably past strenuous squash games. The rot started to set in and LTA suffered many set backs at the hands of very inept and incompetent managers many of whom were imports from the British Isles. The Company became known as "Let's try again" which was a pity as it was once a great outfit. I understand that LTA was sold to Grinaker Construction a while ago. I did however learn a great deal about Construction and the things that can go wrong that end up costing huge sums of money. I believe that construction is like a great Symphony and has to be held together by a single overall conductor and everything is brought together in the correct order to create a wonderful space. It seldom happens like this however and the greatest cock-ups known to man are created within the building industry. I have met many wonderful people within the industry and some complete assholes whose egos are bigger than the job that they need to do.

My first six months of work started in the Pay Office, the Pay Master was a little Englishman called Mr. Wilmot and with his big round spectacles was owl like in appearance. He was ably assisted by Mr Singh and Mr Maharajah both incredibly accurate and quick, and of course old James a

Mozambique born African man, fluent in Portuguese, English and a number of African tongues, including Zulu. I suppose in these modern times James would have held the title of Human Resources manager as he was our link to the African Labourers. There was also James the driver, and both James's were gentlemen to the core. I spent many happy hours in their company as they would tell tales of their lives like only African's can. Old James had been with the company from before the war, almost from the beginning really, and he knew all the main players in the company. There was also a young Indian whose name I forget. By Wednesday of every week the time sheets came in, the wage sheets were drawn up, and a wage breakdown was submitted to the bank for delivery early on Thursday morning. The sealed boxes of cash were delivered by a security company and were ceremoniously opened by Mr Wilmot when the cash was checked and signed for. The hundreds of wage envelopes were ready all hand written the day before and the counting out of money began. Mr Wilmot sat in the middle with me and the young Indian sat at either end of a big table. The money for a wage packet was counted by Mr Wilmot, and then passed to one of us, one to the left and one to the right. We then checked and packed the money leaving the packet open in case we did not balance and we could re-check each one. It was a tedious business but after a while we became quite proficient and accurate. We went through a stage when a number of labourers complained of being short in their pay. This was always put right but not long afterwards Mr Wilmot caught my young Indian colleague helping himself by dropping a few notes onto his lap instead of into the wage packet. Mr Wilmot exploded into action, puffing himself up to his full 5 feet 3 inches he took the chap by the ear and threw him out of the office. I suppose the temptation of all that money was just too much but as he and I had become quite friendly I felt very let down that he had done such a thing. Anyway by late on Thursday evening all the wages were packed back into steel containers one for each contract, collected by the security company and delivered to each site early on Friday Morning. Mr Wilmot would set off by car to pay all the out lying sites and we would set off on foot starting at John Ross House, then back across to 320 West Street, then Woolworths, then Durdoc Centre and finally The General Accident Insurance Company. Between Woolworths and Durdoc Centre there was a small job at the Natal Mercury News Paper. The wages for this site were in the Woolworths Security Box and we would walk from Woolworths about a block to this site with the pockets of our Safari Suits bulging with wage packets. Imagine doing that nowadays!!

My next stint was in the buying office, where every day hundreds of orders would come in from the different sites. There was a head buyer, and three buyers and a trainee. The first few hours of every morning were very hectic with every item was needed yesterday it seemed but generally by lunchtime we had everything sorted for delivery from various building supply companies. Of course some people were easier to deal with than others. I was once asked to source a specific size of washer for a brass hose fitting, and I tried every known shop without success. The order had come from a Contracts Manager called Johnny Barns, a tall man with a long beard, a man who had come up through the ranks and was highly respected by his peers and in the industry. I made the mistake of reporting back that I had failed in my quest to obtain the washes. Well did I get a rollicking, he told me that if we couldn't get what they wanted then we should give the order books to the site people and they would do their own buying. I redoubled my efforts and obtained the washers and never ever gave up on a difficult order again. On another occasion I received a call from Trevor Flanagan the Contracts Manager at 320 West Street. The order was for, a rubber hammer, a bevelled edge chalk line and a bag of 6" nails. Now 6" nails are not widely used, rubber mallets are available but not hammers, and a bevelled edge chalk line, what was the man on about?? I took the order down then went through to Peter Hawyes one of the buyers and said that I thought Trevor Flanagan had lost his marbles and started to relate the order to him. Half way through he could no longer contain his mirth and confessed to placing the order himself. After spending some time in the accounts department I began my site experience.

Now it has to be said that Southern Africa is a gem in the worlds crown for its beauty is beyond compare and no matter what catastrophes are taking place around you growing up there was a privilege. Although the system was perhaps unfair and our lifestyle unrealistic people got on, there was a great deal of kindness between the races and we grew up in a kind of paradise. Later in the 80's and 90's black on black violence reached epic proportions and unbelievable savagery became commonplace. But even with all the instability and now having experienced life in Europe and Asia I think that we were still better off. The test of time will be if the black majority are better off now that they are "free" or is it all going to end in tears. Bishop Tutu said the most sensible thing ever on the Opra Winfrey Show, when he suggested that the women must take over. The same applies in other male dominated societies like Arabia, and India and Asia. Women need to take control of their lives and eventually the destiny of their people and families. Let's face it the thousands of years of male domination and rule has been an abysmal failure so let's try something new. Anyway I digress, back to Smith Street in Durban.

One Sunday morning I called in at General Accident Building where Cliffy Davies was busy installing the two layers of pre-cast panels that adorn the building on the first and second podium floors. I had spent the morning on the beach and was driving down Smith Street on my way home but decided to call in to see how the work was progressing. The panels had reached the corner of the building and Cliff and I were on the podium when at exactly 12 Noon when there was a huge noise like an explosion and the crane on our Bay Passage site that was diagonally opposite us collapsed into the concrete lift core. I have never seen anything like it as dust and debris billowed out of every opening in the concrete core of the shaft. The crane was being lifted at the time when the lifting jack sheared and down it came. Sadly one of the lifting crew went down with it and it took until midnight on the following Tuesday night to dig his body out. The concrete counterweight that collapsed with tremendous force into the wall of the core punched a hole through fifteen inches of reinforced concrete. High-rise construction is a risky business but some sites seem more prone to have fatalities than others and at least six people lost their lives on the Bay Passage building all in freak accidents. This very crane was previously used on the medical centre contract in Pietermaritzburg before being used at Bay Passage and the boom had collapsed across the deck there killing some labourers. I can still remember our new managing director, a very self-opinionated man called Jeff Bowden, boasting about what a hero he had been at the inquest.

A firm of Quantity Surveyors in Johannesburg called

Hickman Bjorkman and Bower had been employed to look after the interests of the client who were the General Accident Insurance Company. Des Bower offered me a position in his firm where I began work in September 1976. In December that year I married Katherine and we set up home in a bachelor flat on the 18th Floor of Rennie House in Hoofd Street in Braamfontein, Johannesburg. I had made my own double bed in knock down form, which I wrapped in a sleeping bag and loaded onto the roof wracks of my Fiat 1100, drove up to my new life and job on Sunday afternoon but I couldn't raise the caretaker. This meant that I had to proceed to the East Rand to stay with friends and return on the Monday Morning. My first night in my new home was spent sleeping on the floor, the entire front was glass windows and we had an electrical storm the flashed and thundered at me through the glass. It was an incredible display to welcome me to the highveld.

Life continued and my first born son Michael arrived against the flow of modern contraception, born at about 1.30pm at the Mary Mount Maternity Hospital near Bez Valley in Johannesburg. At 3.25kg he was the biggest baby there until Moaner Van Heerden's wife delivered their first born who unsurprisingly enough was a good bit bigger. Moaner was one of the great South African locks who never got to experience proper international competition due to the sport boycott that was in force at the time. It was a difficult 15 hour labour that ended with Dr Rothschild the gynaecologist using forceps to ease Michael out into the world. There was a lot of pushing and screaming and blood and the little nurse nun dug me in the ribs and said look your babies coming as the head crowned. It was all very strange and wonderful.

Once Michael arrived our wings were clipped and we left Johannesburg, making several moves around the country and after quite a long spell in Pietermaritzburg we found ourselves settled in the farming dorp (Town) of Ladysmith, in Natal. It was the policy of the government of the day to build factories in rural areas and to offer incentives to industrialists to open the factories and so provide the local populace with work. Many thousands of square metres of factories were built during this time and the Ezakheni Industrial Estate was born about 17 km outside of Ladysmith. Ladysmith is a typical small Natal town with small mindedness quite noticeable but it was a wonderful place to raise children, who could roam quite freely and who formed wonderful friendships that survive up to this time.

After enjoying some success with a small construction business things started to go wrong in the late 90's and life became very difficult and it seemed that no matter what we did it turned against us. It became obvious that it was time to move on and with the entire mood felt in the country rather gloomy and a number of friends leaving for Australia and New Zealand, but being seduced by the mighty pound I decided to obtain an Ancestral Visa and left for London in May 2001. I am fairly proud of the fact that in all of my dealings with the African Workforce in my own company and as branch manager of another everyone was treated with respect and honesty and humility and in all of the years working there we had no problems with our staff. I do believe that our attitude to the African people went a long way to ensuring my families protection after I had left for London, as we were not interfered with in any way. Since leaving the country law and order has largely broken down and there is a tidal wave of crime that washes backwards and forwards across the country. Recently an ex neighbour of ours in Ladysmith lost his life to a burglar who shot him in the leg it must be said with his own 9mm pistol and he bled to death before anyone could help him. My son Gareth who found London too restrictive returned to South Africa and lives with his girlfriend in Krugersdorp west of Johannesburg, where all their pets were poisoned, their cat and two dogs died, two dogs survived as they rushed them to the vet as soon as they found them. The criminal element, it has to be said mostly black people have developed a poison called one step two step because when fed to animals they take one step and fall over dying on the second step. In my opinion one would need the intellect of a tick to do something like that, but what intervention, or criticism has there been from the west? Nothing, not a word, it would seem that because the blacks are in control of the country the daily murder of people to steal their possessions is quite acceptable. The governments answer to the black on white plunder is to tell the whites that they should leave if they don't like the way things are. A typical response but where will the country be then, and I would go so far as to suggest that the only thing that prevented the two dominant Inguni tribes from indulging in complete genocide in the so called political violence of the 80's and early 90's was the efforts of the army and police force. This huge clash could still happen, all that is needed is the right ingredients at the right time for the world to witness the greatest slaughter ever seen in humankind's violent history. The world instead is rewarding South Africa by entrusting the 2010 world cup to the country, a decision that in my opinion needs some serious review.

David Rattray, a well known raconteur and historian and also one of the biggest supporters of the once great Zulu Nation was murdered in his home and business by Zulu thugs. I had exchanged e-mails with him just before leaving for London, expressing my concerns for the future and his reply was up beat saying that South Africa had always lurched from one crisis to another and he was optimistic about the future. Well they've killed him as well.

The Zulu wars of 1879 should never have happened and came about due to the meeting of two cultures one "civilised" and one "savage" and the huge misunderstandings that followed and still do plague the peaceful co-existence of African and European people. My wife's great uncle was Lt Raw who when scouting with the native contingent at Isandhlwana, came upon the 20000 strong Zulu army, an event that precipitated the start of the battle on that fateful day in January 1879, the worst defeat ever suffered by the British army, by a savage foe armed largely with shields and spears. By the end of the day 1349 British officers and men lay dead, along with about 3000 Zulu's.

The 6th February 1985 will forever be etched in my mind for two reasons. I had enjoyed an evening of sensational love making the night before with my wife, one of those exceptional couplings when the earth moves for both of you and I had never been more in love with her. At 6.40am on the morning of the 6th February 1985, I was driving to work on my usual route happily reflecting on our nocturnal adventure when I was involved in a head on collision that would have killed most men. The road passes through a steep cutting on a slight uphill turning to the right. As I approached there was an articulated lorry at the crest of the rise and on the left of the lorry in the grass verge travelling at full ahead was a dreaded E20 mini bus taxi. There were great clouds of sand, dust and pebbles being thrown up on either side of the vehicle. My first reaction was that something was horribly wrong and my decision to slow down was my undoing. On passing the lorry the mini bus driver swerved back across a kerb onto the tarmac, the back wheels becoming airborne in the process. It landed pointing diagonally across my path and was heading for the sloping wall of the cutting. Realising her mistake she then swerved back directly into my path still going at full ahead. My last thought was "I don't believe this is happening" then an almighty bang and then blackness.

The statistics were one dead and fourteen injured. The impact was huge enough to turn the minibus onto its roof, which resulted in horrific injuries as all of the passengers were thrown out onto the road. The mini bus was carrying African nursing sisters from the township to the Provincial Hospital in Town. Shortly after the impact I came to inside the wreckage of my car, which was threatening to ignite, the Taxi was upside down in front and to the right of my location and there were bodies strewn about. The sister that was killed was laying half in and half out of where the windscreen had been, her dress torn up passed her waist, she was wearing cheap Pep store panties and she was staring straight at me. She had a huge wound on her forehead and her lips were drawn across her teeth in a grimace of death. My life would never be the same after this and I spent the next four months in hospital tied to an aluminium frame with both legs in traction, my left hip smashed in half, my right femur splintered into slithers of bone, my right arm broken in two places five broken ribs and a collapsed lung. After the crash I was rushed from the midlands to Pietermaritzburg's Greys Hospital and the nurse that accompanied me in the ambulance told me months later that she didn't think that I would make it. I did I'm still here and even fathered my beautiful daughter four years afterwards. The driver of the mini bus taxi was a woman of thirty-four who had passed her driving test two months prior to the accident. Her previous experience of driving a vehicle was probably only limited to the driving schools 1400cc car. On obtaining her licence she was immediately employed to drive up to sixteen people around in a mini bus, a job that she could legally do under South African Law but a job that she was hopelessly unqualified for. She was charged with culpable homicide and we were both still wearing callipers when the court case came around. Although she was found guilty she was freed without penalty as the magistrate said that she had suffered enough. She even left the court with her driving licence still valid.

The sister that died in the accident had two children and I often wonder how they got on after their mother never came home that day.

I first met Michael Murray in 1983 when we moved to Ladysmith to build factories and we needed tradesmen rather urgently. Limit Hill is the township on the outskirts of town where the coloureds live (olive skinned lively people of mixed race), and as there are many very capable trades' people among this group. I began my search by knocking on the door of a neat bungalow the first in the street, a young man came to the door and so began a friendship and working relationship that spanned many years. Michael trained as a carpenter in Umtata in the Cape and he was incredibly neat and accurate, his work was of the highest standard. There are some incredible buildings that he supervised that look as good to-day as they did when they were handed over to the clients, but Michael was shot and killed in an ambush about three months before I left to work in England. Michael was a magnificent man a gentle man, quiet and unassuming. Michael had lived in Ladysmith Natal for nearly thirty years and his sudden death shocked the coloured community. The church was packed for his funeral and my wife and his immediate work colleague and I were the only white people present. "Birds of a feather" is one thing but I thought this was really poor. Mike if you are out there, think of me in the freezing cold of England.

The apartheid system in South Africa left a deep scar on Michael and although never outspoken he carried a deep seated resentment against the marginalising of the coloured people. When his children were young they would park on the road outside the drive-in theatre in Ladysmith to try to glimpse the film that was showing, coloureds not being allowed into the drive-in then. His children would ask him why they couldn't go inside to see the film, so how does one explain to a child that the colour of your skin precludes you from watching a film. Years later when things became more relaxed and all were welcome Michael refused to set foot in the place.

In the same week that Michael was murdered a lady specialist paediatrician who had dedicated her life to helping black children, was shot and killed in tribal trust areas, and a 90 year old catholic priest was killed for his vehicle. What do these people hope to achieve with these senseless attacks.

Chapter Seven

Byfleet

It was with some trepidation that I kissed my wife of twenty-four and a half years goodbye at Jan Smuts's airport and together with my twenty two-year-old son boarded an Air Gabon flight via Libreville to London. The aircraft reminded me of a very old E-20 minibus as two toilets didn't work and the luggage storage doors were hanging by their hinges. The landing gear made a terrible groaning sound as it retracted. The picture of a sweating Zulu somewhere in the bowels of the plane cranking it up by hand crossed my mind. We landed in Libreville at 10.00 p.m. and walked into a wall of heat which lasted until we went into the airport building which was just a little cooler. Gabon's currency is worse than ours is and I got quite a lot of whatever they have there for R10.00. We shared a warm beer before boarding the plane bound for Gatwick England. We landed at 6.00am on a crisp cool summer morning. After clearing customs we made our way to Putney where my niece lives. We only had one close call when my wheeled suitcase nearly slid off the passenger landing at the back of the bus. Luckily my son is young and quick and managed to grab hold of the handle before all was lost. After a shower and a cup of coffee I made my way to Southend on Sea where I had arranged to stay with a friend. After a barbecue and a few beers, I retired to bed ready to fight another day in the morning.

I was going to start work in Wimbledon and so I made my way there to look for accommodation. Armed with the "Loot" newspaper, a large publication of advertisements for anyone looking for anything in London, a travel pass, and a London A-Z I set off. Probably because my wife is an excellent cook and due to my natural aversion to exercise I arrived in London in a very overweight and unfit condition. I learned this day that London is not the place for middle-aged overweight adventurers. The English, an un-accommodating lot at best, do not like fat people and tend to look at you askance. Most Londoners are fairly trim due to the lifestyle of catching buses and tubes and walking long distances in going about the daily business of making a living. London is also full of staircases. My English cousin who is 76 years old lives four floors up and as a result is extremely fit and he and his wife don't even notice the stairs and I come plodding along later. You get an insight into why the English have never lost a war. Little Tommy Atkins is alive and well and living in London. After walking many miles to look for accommodation from run down to almost a slum, I ended the day with nothing more than sore feet and blisters. The problem it seemed, was that cheap accommodation in London is shared by under thirty year olds who are not about to share it with a middle aged adventurer. A lot of time was wasted until I started to admit my age before setting forth for another long walk. I became very homesick and depressed and I nearly gave up and went home. A young friend of mine with wisdom way beyond his years persuaded me to stay on at least until I had recovered what I had spent on the excursion. My work colleagues were wonderful and after two weeks in the YMCA I moved into a cabin on the building site. This saved my meagre budget and I felt a little happier.

Wimbledon is full of little pubs and restaurants and the odd nightclub. Many South Africans live in Wimbledon shoulder to shoulder with Australians, Kiwis, Pakistanis and the odd Englishman. Chumbley's bar, now a walkabout pub, opposite the Flaming Wok comes alive with sport mad South Africans on days when South Africa plays sport against anyone. They stock Castle Lager, five for ten pounds a bargain at R30.00 each all spread out in a silver ice bucket and covered with ice. It makes a great advert for S A Breweries. When the boys sing Die Stem and Nkosi Sikelela Africa they raise the roof and you realise that everyone there is homesick and knows that for better or for worse the way of life as we knew it is gone forever. The beer flows, the game begins and the party is on.

Andy, a work colleague of mine whose father was a Royal Marine R S M and who fought with the Ghurkha Regiments during World War two, is a tough little character who spends half of his time in England and half of his time in France where he is refurbishing some houses. Andy left to go back to France and so the boys went out on the town. We ended up in the Poo Na Na club, also known as the ooh la la club, which was noisy and dark. As gentlemen don't get drunk they only get tired- and we were all quite tired at this stage-I did my usual trick and fell asleep. The place was crowded with blearing music and Mick couldn't believe it when people near me were telling others to shush so as not to wake me up. All good things come to an end and I left Wimbledon for the head office in Byfleet. The search for accommodation continued and Angela, a work colleague who has tremendous local knowledge, took me under her wing. Angela took me to see a sweet old lady friend who was renting a room with its own bathroom in her beautifully furnished home. After an interview she decided not to take me in because of my size and she told Angela that I may break her furniture. Clearly I am far grosser than I ever imagined. Sadly good food, good wine and good company have always been a priority in my life to the detriment of my frame that is prone to expand at the slightest provocation. Plan B was Frank whom Angela was a bit worried about because he had had a nervous breakdown and she felt that he might be a bit unstable. Frank has turned out to be a very kind and thoughtful individual who has just allowed life to get the better of him. He owns a comfortable house in Byfleet and after my experiences of trying to find accommodation I was very grateful to be taken in. Frank holds a Physics degree but has been unable to work for years as a result of his breakdown. Franks day begins somewhere between 11.00am and 1.00pm, when he drags himself out of bed. Four afternoons a week Frank travels up to Brixton where he does voluntary work for World Development Movement a watchdog group that organises protests against Corporate Giants that step out of line. In the evenings Frank plays bridge, chess, or badminton with various friends or social groups. Whatever time Frank gets in he logs onto the internet and plays chess until the early hours of the morning, sometimes only retiring at 6.00am.

Angela who as I mentioned is a great organiser went to Amsterdam to visit her sister. She took John along. John is a family friend of long standing who at the age of sixty six admitted that he was still a virgin but after a visit to the Red Light District decided that he may like to alter his status. No problem for Angela, she helped John select the girlie, negotiated the £30.00 fee, (for which the lady was prepared to take them both on), Angela waited in the coffee shop across the street. The girl was a real professional as John was back in the coffee shop in twelve minutes. Every dog has its day I suppose but imagine loosing your virginity at the age of 66 in a whorehouse in Amsterdam.

Because I had the use of a company car, Frank and I would generally go touring to various places of interest on the southern coastline. Unfortunately wherever you go especially in summer thousands of people seem to have got there before you. Playing in the traffic is a way of life here and the M 25, an eight-lane highway that circumnavigates London, is known as the world's biggest parking lot as it often comes to a complete standstill.

One weekend I drove down to visit Mr Maber in Martock in Somerset. Mr Maber is the local historian and genealogist and is an incredibly interesting man. He is one of the survivors of the H.M.S. Eagle a carrier that was sunk during World War Two. Martock is a quaint little town in which two generations of my ancestors lived and worked there as General Practitioners and their old home and surgery which is now a national monument is occupied by a retired Royal Navy Commander and his wife. Because it was summer holidays the traffic was wild and it took me five hours to get down there. The road passes Stonehenge and it was quite interesting to see it standing there up on the hill. In Martock I was able to visit the ancestral graves of Richard Martyn Westcott and Peter Westcott, and visit the church in which they no doubt worshipped. The people who now occupy the old home and surgery were not in so I couldn't visit there.

The 11/9/2001 came along and the horrific events of that day, sights and sounds of mayhem on a grand scale. My late mother used to say that every thirty to fifty years someone or something comes along which so evil that the world is forced to take up arms to defend itself. Well Bin Laden has done it now with his brand of radical Islam the world will be too small for him to hide in and he will be hunted down with all of his cronies. England which had immediately responded to the support of America, in actual fact the feeling of outrage, anger, sympathy and grief felt in London and I'm sure across the British Isles was tangible, and at 11.00am on the Friday after the attack we observed a three-minute silence. The sight of these tough working men standing silent at their work areas with heads bowed was a moving moment and one that I shall probably never forget. Later that day I met another Englishman who believed that all the memorial services and church services being offered up around the world were a complete waste of time and uncalled for. He pointed out that when we have a natural disaster like an earthquake or flood with huge loss of life we don't have the same response. This is correct but there is a big difference between falling down the stairs and being pushed down. Although I feel a bit like a refugee here in England the thing is however that if England needed overweight adventurers to serve in an armed force I would happily volunteer and yet if comrade Mandela's South African government wanted to raise an armed force I would be most reluctant. I would never want my sons to serve in any South African Force as the ideology and political leanings of our new leaders are at the opposite ends of the spectrum from my own and the ANC's ties and friendships with some of the worlds dodgiest despots will always be a concern.

Chapter Eight

The Falloons

After having been living in London for a few months, I wrote a letter to the times, which they declined to publish.

Sir,

I am South African and have been living and working in London for five and a half months. There are a number of current topics that I would like to comment on.

This morning on T V was a piece about the English being a Nation of moaners and a chap was interviewed who had written a book about complaining. In South Africa last year 50% of the people who died did so as a result of AIDS related diseases and 50% of the remainder probably died suddenly and violently.

Earlier this week on T V was a story about Albanian orphans who have been brought to England and given some kind of a life. It was so sad you could hardly bear to watch. To-day on T V was a story of black H I V + (positive) orphans being cared for in a home in Johannesburg South Africa, interestingly enough by two white women who appealed for help for drugs and funds to try to give them some kind of a life. One can't help wondering if the various welfare groups feel the same way about black orphans as they do about white ones.

The point is that apart from Rail track and queuing on the M25 England is a wonderful place to be and her people should count their blessings.

Sir, I am South African and have
been living and working in London for
5½ months. There are a number of current
topics that I would like to comment on.
This morning on T.V. was a piece about
the English being a Nation of moaners
and a chap was interviewed who had
written a book about complaining.
In South Africa last year 50% of the
people who died did so as a result
of AIDS related diseases and 50% of the
remainder probably died suddenly and
violently.
    Earlier this week on TV was a
story about Albanian orphans who
have been brought to England and
given some kind of a life. It was so
sad you could hardly bear to watch.
To-day on TV was a story of black HIV+
(positive) orphans being cared for in
a home in Johannesburg South Africa
interestingly enough by two white
women who appealed for help for.
drugs and funds to try to give
them some kind of a life. One
can't help wondering if the various
welfare groups feel the same way
about black orphans as they do about
white ones.
    The point is that apart from

Railtrack and queing on the M25
England is a wonderful place
to be and her people should
count their blessings.

PHILIP GEE
41 FULLERTON ROAD
BY FLEET
SURREY
KT 14 7 TA.

They wrote back.

Dear Mr Gee

*Although we thank you for your letter to the Editor, dated October
17, which was read with interest here, we regret we were unable to
publish it.*

Yours sincerely

Squiggle

Pp Ivan Barnes
Letters Editor

THE TIMES

1 Pennington Street, London E98 1TA
Telephone: 020 7782 5000 Fax: 020 7782 5046 e-mail: letters@thetimes.co.uk

18 October 2001

Mr Philip Gee
41 Fullerton Road
Byfleet
Surrey KT14 7TA

Dear Mr Gee

Although we thank you for your letter to the Editor,
dated October 17, which was read with interest here,
we regret we were unable to publish it.

Yours sincerely

pp Ivan Barnes
    Letters Editor

Registered Office: Times Newspapers limited, 1 Virginia Street, London E98 1XY.
Registered No. 894646 England

The first day Declan Marrinan walked into the open plan office in his lazy style, and introduced himself, I knew that we would get on. The evening before BBC had screened "ZULU" the epic tale of the Zulu Wars, Declan related the story of the Welsh soldiers singing Men of Harloch as the Zulu's advanced, and one of the soldiers said "don't antagonise them sing something they know". At this we broke down laughing much to the disdain of the rather stiff occupants of the office around us. Declan invited me to a Sunday night gig at his local, as by day he is a Contracts Manager and by night plays the Bodhran Drum in a Celtic band called the Falloons. What a great evening the highlight of which was an Irish Folk song sung without accompaniment by Declan and which only an Irishman could do Justice to. It goes like this and would bring a tear to a glass eye.

WE MAY OR MIGHT NEVER ALL MEET HERE AGAIN

My friends and companions come join me in rhyme come lift up your voices in chorus with mine come lift up your voices or agree to refrain for we may or might never all meet here again.

So here's a health to the company and one to my lass lets drink and be merry all out of one glass lets drink and be merry or agree to refrain for we may or might never all meet here again.

So here's a health to the wee lass that I love so well for her style and her beauty there is none can excel. There's a smile on her countenance as she sits upon my knee sure there's no man in this wide world as happy as me.

So here's a health to the company and one to my lass lets drink and be merry all out of one glass lets drink and be merry or agree to refrain for we may or
might never all meet here again.

Our ship lies at anchor she is ready to dock and I wish her safe landing without any shock and if ever I should meet you by land or by sea I will always remember your kindness to me for we may or might never all meet here again.
Copyright

After seven months away, I went home for Christmas and the wonderful heat of Africa. Things at home have not improved and we have decided to move to England. This decision was reinforced as shortly after my return to England in the New Year, Gareth, my younger son walked into an armed robbery and got bashed over the head with a hand gun and tied up with a dustbin over his head. When he wriggled free of the dustbin he had the gun put to his temple and told to be still or be shot. Luckily he was not seriously hurt. Why it is that Africans turn so easily to crime, is it to do with their history of conquest and plunder of other tribes cattle and women.

If the violent crime in Southern Africa cannot be curtailed I predict that Southern Africa's future is precarious and those that suffer the most are the black majority. You can be sure that the ever-lengthening gravy train will grind to a halt, which is the time when the real trouble will start.
As it is I doubt if our leaders loose any sleep about the increasing number of un-employed people and the number of company's that are closing down. Are we in South Africa going to end up like our Northern Neighbour's in Zimbabwe? Comrade Bob's recent purge of shanty town

that had sprung up in Harare, and on TV the picture of that magnificent young man sitting on the edge of an iron bed in the open the ruins of his home around him and a look of utter despair on his great black face. Does no one care?

Comrade Bob Mugabe of Zimbabwe, having managed to wangle his way to power after a Zimbo election, drove to the opening of Parliament in an open backed Vintage Rolls Royce with Mrs Bob in all her splendid garb next to him and of all things a guard of honour of mounted lancers. Comrade Bob, a Communist who hates the Brits, (actually everyone I think), embracing the colonial past. How confusing! Perhaps he thinks he is sticking his finger up the noses of his old masters, England. One would think a more traditional mode of transport would be more appropriate but then this is Africa that we are talking about. One thing I have learned in my short time in England is that by and large the west does not give a fig about Africa especially despots like Comrade Bob. The cock up there is clearly the fault of the British Colonialists who provided the infrastructure enjoyed by Zimbabwe, and after forcing Ian Smith to hand over power to Mugabe, left without paying him anything for compensation. What a lovely mess they have made of things there, and now they are leaning on China to help them out of the mire. That will be an interesting contest when the time comes.

Nkosi Sikelela iAfrica. (God Bless Africa)

Jason James and Daniel Whyte received a total of eight life sentences for the cold blooded murder of a Hoddesdon millionaire's wife, seriously wounding his son and his son's girlfriend during a robbery in which her and her husbands Rolex watches were stolen. James stood over his victim and removed the watch as she lay in agony. Driving to work one morning I heard the report on the radio and took in the very English sounding names I thought what absolute brutes these boys must be. The next day I bought the Hoddesdon and Broxbourne Mercury when all was revealed with the black faces of Jason James and Daniel Whyte staring out from the front page. Mr. Justice Bell said: "It is difficult to imagine a more lawless and heartless crime than the murder of Mrs. Martorana." They have received minimum 25 and 20 year sentences which mean that they will be freed when they are in their early and mid fifties and you can be sure that they will do more of the same. In my opinion they should never be freed. The difference is that in England these criminals are pursued and eventually convicted for their crimes unlike the situation in Southern Africa. Do you suppose that the murderers of the Zimbabwe farmer who became famous in death because of his faithful dog that was curled up asleep on the blanket that covered his corpse will ever be prosecuted? Not likely!!

At the moment here in England there is a lot of talk about Africa and saving the children and Bob Geldoff is doing another concert called "live 8". There has been trouble in Ethiopia, which was quelled, in the usual brutal style by shooting all the protesters dead. Bob was on TV last night bemoaning the fact but it's time Bob understood that this is the catastrophe of what Africa is and always has been. Bob would be better off putting his energy into problems at home like the poor standard of education, yobs and yob culture, what can be done about saving these youngsters from a life of drudgery and ignorance? George W. has caught on with his plan to only help the African countries whose governments tow the line, and in time Africa may even develop into something worthwhile. But George W is also letting the side down with his support of the oil rich

Equatorial Guinea and its despotic leader and his son. Even if the crazy coup attempt there hadn't failed all it would have done was replace one despot with another.

My younger son Gareth was 16 when I left for the UK and I knew that it was the worst possible time. He was a model child up to this point, but he reacted very badly to my leaving and got into all kinds of scrapes and fights that were just not him. Gareth is in Matric (Form 10) now and has done very well considering that he suffered from Attention Deficit Disorder as a youngster. He has grown out of his learning disability and has become a very good swimmer. As I am in England and he is at home with his mother and grandmother relations have become a bit strained between them all and Gareth wants to move out. Gareth was selected to swim in five events at the South African Junior swimming champs in Pretoria but he has decided that he is no longer interested in swimming or staying at home with his mother; he just wants to gap it. How do you offer advice long range as he told me the other day that as I don't live there anymore I don't know what its like? I have been married a long time and knowing my mother in law as I do I can hazard a guess. I sent Gareth a fax.

My Dear Gareth,

I know that you are upset and angry at the moment but I want you to read this letter very carefully and more than once. At present your whole world is within restricted boundaries. What you need to understand is that the world is very big and at your feet. In the world there are winners and losers. The winners shrug off their disappointments and look for new adventures while the losers get grumpy and angry and lose more.

You do not realise how much swimming talent you have. You have the perfect shape and endless strength. To move from the level that you are at to National standard would not take much. At the S A Junior's there are bound to be selectors looking for future talent for the National side. You have it within your grasp.

I want you to go back to swimming today and ask Ivan to train you for the S A Juniors. Train twice a day so that when you get there you are in explosive form.

Please don't let this opportunity go past.

I love you. Dad.

You give your children so much but you cannot live their lives for them. Who was it that said that youth is wasted on the young? Here I am at fifty years old, making my way in a very different environment poorer than I have been for years but much happier. I often think of friends that I had who didn't make it, Sven aged eighteen killed in a car crash in the early 70's and Phil Tuck in his late 20's killed in 77 with his young wife at the wheel. Are these events really decreed, written in some divine journal God only knows where?

Chapter Nine

LUD

I needed transport when I came back to England in January 02 and so I bought "LUD" a 1989 Austin Montego Estate with 105,000 miles on the clock. When it needed some minor repair I took it in and the garage man said, "Well there is good news and bad news, the bad news is that it is the most undesirable car in England but the good news is that they go for ever and no one will ever steel it." I paid £125.00 for "LUD" and covered 30,000 miles in her before giving her up to the scrap merchants. The English have an absolute love affair with big powerful cars, which is ridiculous when you consider the time that it takes to go anywhere and the amount of traffic. The average time to cover 100miles in the South East is probably two and a half hours. The number of road accident deaths seems to be on the up and driving around you notice little shrines of flowers and crosses, some even with the victims photograph to mark the spot of their demise. Statistically and actually the standard of driving in the U K is very good mostly with considerate and law abiding drivers on the roads. The problem is that most roads are very narrow here and set down into a kind of earth channel with moss and fern covered banks each side and combined with the speed factor available in modern cars road deaths are here to stay. I worked for a highway maintenance company for a time and one day on the way back to the office we witnessed the most dramatic crash that I have ever seen. As usual it was raining and as we drove out of a roundabout into a dual carriageway I noticed the car coming towards us start to wobble and I said to my colleague look at this, the next thing the car was air borne, turning sideways in the air then spinning like a top at least three times before smashing down on to its roof and over to rest on its undercarriage, as all the wheels had been ripped off. The driver was alive but had what appeared to be severe head injuries. Three fire engines attended the scene and he was gently extricated from the wreck and taken to hospital in an air ambulance. As the driver seemed to us to be more than a little bit drunk he will be faced with the prospect of a long ban and having to pay for a car that is now wrecked. Luckily for him he was the only one hurt.

Anyway "LUD" as she became known because of the last letters of registration, served me well for fourteen months and only let me down once when she ran out of petrol one cold and wet winters evening on the M25 just before Heathrow airport on the anticlockwise side. I managed to coast to the side of the road but what a nightmare with the wake of huge lorries shaking "LUD" every time they thundered past. The AA rescued me that night and saw me on my way. Later that night I was wandering around Tesco's looking for something to eat when I got a call from the police asking if I had got off the M25 O K, a very civilised act I thought. Another incident, which involved the police and "LUD" and I am ashamed to say me, was when I was arrested for the first time in my life. I have kept in contact with Declan my Irish mate and was in the habit of wandering down to the Kings Head in Rudgwick to have a few beers after work. English beer is very palatable and it was one of those evenings that time forgot and we drank to closing time. Although I felt the effect of the alcohol I was mentally fine and wandered off in search of a hamburger from the kebab wagon but I was too late and the kebab wagon

wasn't there. Continuing on my way just before I got to the M3 the blue lights lit up behind me and I drew up to the verge. The reason that I was pulled over was that I hadn't washed "LUD" since I had bought her a year before and they couldn't read my number plate. Of course they smelt my breath and I was asked to blow in the breathalyser. I was over the legal limit and so was taken into custody by two young policemen. "LUD" was driven off and parked somewhere out of harms way. Because of my accent I had to admit my heritage "Oh really said policeman No. 1 its our time for South Africans we picked up a whole car load last night." I can just imagine that particular scene. Anyway they were incredibly kind to me and after being processed at Woking police station was sent on my way in the early hours of the morning. It transpired that I was very close to the legal limit of 0.035ml and so I wasn't charged. It was all so civilised it was almost enjoyable and I told the young policemen when they dropped me off that I couldn't have been arrested by two nicer people. Somewhat different from the treatment metered out to a friend of ours in South Africa who had volunteered to marshal a fun run around our little town in Ladysmith. He was at his post absent-mindedly finishing a can of Castle Lager when a Police van appeared and he was unceremoniously thrown into the back by an Indian and black constable. They drove to the police station at break neck speed where he was thrown into a cell. The charge was drinking in a public place. Pay back time is probably quite enjoyable for some South Africans at the moment but I would warn them not to push too hard as they may waken a sleeping giant and the greatest white tribe of all Africa may rise up and re-colonise the homeland. I do believe that eventually Africa will be in such a sorry state that intervention from more sophisticated countries will become normal procedure. I am sure that some sort of partnering arrangement could be worked out with proper structures in place to stop despots like comrade Bob getting hugely rich while the country flounders around in a state of chaos. Compare his position to Tony Blair, who in my opinion doesn't do a bad job, is severely criticised by the left, right and centre, works all the hours God gave him to run one of the worlds strongest economies and all for a very moderate amount of money while an incompetent like comrade Bob has reduced his country to ruin but got wealthy along the way. One thing that the colonials proved was that when African Countries are properly run there is enough to go around,

Zambia being a case in point was handed back by Britain as a going concern but was reduced to ruin within twenty years. Zambia had a vibrant economy as strong as South Africa's and now the place is run by a kind of underground African style Mafia and you will not do business there unless you are in the club. There are huge areas in Zambia that are largely unpopulated, as whole communities have been wiped out by the AIDS virus. There are parts that are so beautiful it's as if they received a special blessing from the creator himself. Barotseland in western Zambia is one such place where the great Zambisi River runs from North to South until it reaches the Victoria Falls and then thunders on from west to east to the coast. For hundreds of years the Lozi people have lived on the flood plains of this great river moving to higher ground when the wet season starts and the Bulozi becomes a giant lake. The royal household is transported to high ground on a large wooden barge painted with black and white stripes and propelled by paddlers standing down each side. Where the Lozi's learnt the art of boat building is another of Africa's mysteries, but the beating of drums the day before heralds the Kuomboka ceremony that is held annually. The paddlers are required to paddle in time to a drumbeat and any man who missed a beat was thrown overboard and eaten by crocodiles. This practice continues to modern times, the difference being that the unfortunate is picked up in a boat following along behind.

Anyway again I ramble, back to old England where we are in mid summer. When the sun shines here it is the most beautiful place in the world with the most amazing wild flowers that spring up all over the fields. My family joined me here in Feb '03 and are slowly settling down. We have rented a 16th century cottage in the village of Holyborne that in by gone times was on the main route from Southampton to London. Most of the main routes that are followed today, which lead to London, were old Roman Roads and a few hundred yards from where we live is a historic Roman Site. I can imagine that when the Romans landed here all those years ago they found the locals to be unpredictable uneducated savages, (some still are) much the same as more recently when the Dutch and the Portuguese landed in sub equatorial Africa. Four hundred years on and Africa is well on its way back to being the wild and untamed continent that it has always been. Dr Livingston's dream of the three "C's" Civilisation, Christianity and Commerce are well and truly out of the window, but perhaps in another two thousand years?

I have now been in England for four years and so have qualified to apply for indefinite leave to stay in the UK. In another year, after singing "God Save The Queen" and swearing allegiance to the crown I will be able to apply for a British Passport. I will be very proud of that document and the fact that I have been able to set up a home from scratch, hold down some tough jobs, be competitive and also be able to contribute in the workplace. In some ways England is more of a jungle than Africa as the general attitude of people here is quite aggressive and selfish, and there is no sense of community and people appear to have no time for one another. Yet at times of great strife like the

Tsunami the British gave more than anyone else it is a bit of a contradiction as on the face of it they come across as quite mean spirited. Abortion is massive as women here are using abortion as a means of contraception and thousands of foetuses are removed every year. This is really scary in that it means that every year upwards of one hundred thousand women are indulging in unprotected sex with unknown partners and these are only the ones that fall pregnant how many others are risking death in this way? Apart from the emotional trauma of having an abortion have they not heard of the HIV Aids virus? I believe that my late mother would be appalled at what in some areas, England has become, legions of young people released into the world at 16 with a GCSE qualification which in a lot of cases means they are barely literate, the general don't care attitude that seems to prevail and a complete lack of respect for themselves and others. Just look at the streets littered with gum and the regular vandalising of public amenities and spaces by brain dead yobs, and the use of vile language in public areas so that all can hear, young and old and endure the anti social abuse. You only have to visit a pub and watch young people eat to realise that they have never been taught to use a knife and fork and have probably never sat down to a meal as a family.

One of my contracts was in Peckham in South London that has a massive black population and so I felt quite at home. The South London people are lovely warm-hearted, party animals and I have grown very fond of this area of London. I worked with Sean and Alan and it was just like working with Rodney and Del Boy from "Only Fools and Horses". They taught me about Pie mash and liquor, and jellied eels, and what the area was like when they were growing up before the housing associations saw fit to flood the Old Kent Road area with black immigrants and there is quite a lot of tension as the area has become a bit unkempt and undesirable. Those that could afford it have moved further out towards Croydon and Bromley. We had a ground worker on site called dodgy Dave because of his rather shady past but what a life he has had. Dave or AKA "SCUD" is thirty-five years old and has the haunted hunted look about him of a wounded animal as from the age of 17 to 24 he spent 35 days outside of prison. There is a thing called the "happy bus" that collects prisoners at the end of their sentence and drives them to a processing centre where all their possessions are returned to them before they are freed. The Old Bill wait for and stop the bus during its journey with a list of new charges for some and its a case of you, you and you come with us please and they the unfortunates are rearrested and charged for other felonies. His last stretch of three years and nine months was for aggravated racial assault on a black man who had beaten up one of his mates. They followed the man from some shops, grabbed him and locked him in the boot of his own car and Dave was busy reversing the vehicle into a brick wall when the Old Bill arrived. Dave, who lives on one of the toughest estates in South London with an older woman, who just happens to be the local Cocaine agent, Dave is her protection, her runner, and collection agent. His previous girlfriend is incarcerated for murdering another woman after an argument about some borrowed clothes. Cocaine is freely available all over London and relatively cheap, as the demand has increased over the last few years. Sex after taking Cocaine is apparently very heightened and combined with Viagra mind blowing. Anyway back to Dave who as I have said spent a lot of time at her majesties pleasure, is as it happens one of the nicest people that I have ever met a real nice guy and speaks about his life with an air of resignation. The time spent in prison was not wasted, as he is very well read, intelligent with an amazing general knowledge. The nickname "SCUD" came about because like the scud missile he is quite reliable but not that accurate and on one hit the following happened. A particular shop owner owed money to a loan shark and Scud and one other were dispatched to deliver a stern warning to the gentleman. The shop was the second one in a particular arcade and Scud ran in with a gallon of varnish splashed it over the stock and then into the face of the astonished man, issued the warning then ran back to the car and jumped into the already open boot of the getaway car. Hit man number two then went back to the shop and told the quivering shopkeeper that if he didn't pay up far worse would happen. "You are the second person to tell me that today stammered the man but it isn't me, that mans shop is at the other end of the arcade." They had hit the wrong one but word got out and the man paid pretty quickly. Protection here is big business and bodyguards hire themselves out at £45 an hour as our company had need of them after a run in with a particularly nasty individual who threatened bodily harm to the directors and certain employees.

It is worth mentioning Dave's life story as compared to my own rather sheltered one it is so horrendous it belies belief. Dave's mother was an Irish girl who already had two children and after a holiday in Majorca found herself expecting a child. Dave was left in the hospital for adoption and in due time was adopted by a couple who hadn't been able to have their own. His "father" was an executive with Lucas auto electrics and quite well off. As often happens not long afterwards mom and dad conceived their own child and Dave I suppose was less of an attraction. His sister was showered with expensive gifts, and Dave who was obviously a bit of a tyke was returned to the social welfare at the age of eleven. I mean how tough is that and the next three years were spent running away from one children's home after another. At the age of 14 the welfare set him up in his own council flat and thus began his baptism into the underworld. I know this sounds incredible but this is how things are in "civilisation".

And now as I write, the London tube system is attacked by home grown terrorists, people that the English proudly insist are English, but are they? Their roots and ideologies come from another place altogether, far removed from England.

A fifty year old man, the son of our old GP in Ladysmith, had his left leg blown off above the knee in the Edgware Road blast, an instant of madness that will alter his life forever. David, an extremely fit long distance runner, left South Africa twenty five years ago, partly in protest to the system there, finds himself a victim of new craziness. But the human spirit does not easily submit and after we visited him in hospital we found that he was very positive and looking forward to trying his prosthetic leg. He was also looking forward to the London Olympic Games as Ken Livingstone has promised that the survivors of the bombings are given front row seats. After the blast and being brought to St Mary's hospital he was attended to by a young anaesthetist who, by pure chance is the daughter of his father's ex partner in their South African medical practice. During the South African Apartheid troubles she and her brother also a doctor, were attending a church service in Cape Town as young interns when the church was attacked by Pan African Congress Terrorists. A Russian seaman near to them had both his legs blown off when a grenade thrown into the church landed in his lap.

Another grenade was smothered by a young man who dived over it taking the full impact of the blast a brave selfless act that saved many lives. Twelve people died that night and there were many injuries and would have been many more save that one member of the congregation who was armed returned the fire hitting one of the terrorists and they withdrew running away from the carnage. The young interns were able to assist in the aftermath. The minister's wife was one of the first to die in a hail of AK47 bullets. Later at the truth and reconciliation hearing the African Terrorist that took her life asked to be forgiven by the minister. He said to him that he could not forgive him as only God can do that. While I respect this man's deep devotion and trust in God, we must also consider the real possibility that there is no God and any spirituality that we feel is within our own heads, wired into the brain.

Chapter Ten

Revelation

Recently I read a book written by a South African Professor, David Lewis Williams, the book is called "The Mind in the Cave" and in time I believe will prove its worth as a revelation of the history of man and the origin of religion that led later on to religious domination of one kind or another. A lifetime of teaching is reflected in the pages and in my opinion it is like having a magic trick revealed as it all seems so obvious. This book should be translated into every language and used as a set work in high schools so that everyone can be aware of the evolution of man from a time when men roamed wild and free into the ruthless, greedy and somewhat ridiculous predator that roams today. People must realise that there is no external force telling us what to do and that we are alone on our little planet and we need to work together to sustain this little world or in the blink of an eye it may no longer exist. In another million years or so some modern life form will no doubt excavate what is left of our planet, sifting through our residual and try to understand how Homo Sapiens Sapiens, succeeded in destroying their world so completely. Our violent past that persists to this day even after all of the breathtaking discoveries and breakthroughs in science and technology we find ourselves drawn into nationalistic tribalism. People are not only drawn to, but worst of all, follow en mass various rabid, egotistical loonies who decide to impose their crazed will on others, always resulting in unspeakable violence. It has to stop. Even with all of the evidence supporting evolution the Creationists cling with white knuckles to the six days and six nights and on the seventh day he rested ideal. Like a time in history when scientists were suggesting that the world was round, no one would believe them and poor old Gallileo had to renounce his theory. And so like the flat earth society, the Creationists continue to ignore the evidence and deny reason believing that mankind is only a few thousand years old and God is responsible for all things.

So here we are two hundred years later as I write this down in my little cottage in Holybourne I wonder what the honourable Richard Martyn Westcott would have thought of the actions and passions of men from the late 1800's until now. I wonder what he would have thought of a dim distant relative who having found his manuscript has included it in a little book, and I wonder what he would have made of Plot 946, North Cann House the first on the road from Plymouth that survives to this day and also the old Oak tree under which he would sit and read some little book. His old home and surgery in Martock that proudly sports a blue national monuments plaque; and the fact that his beloved nephew William Wynn Westcott was suspected in recent times of being Jack the Ripper. What would he have thought of once Great countries like Russia reduced to ruin by the idiocy of their modern day systems and leaders, with extreme suffering and poverty the norm rather than the exception. Thousands of young women forced overseas to become mail order brides or prostitutes in wealthy western and Arab countries. What would he have thought of Ghandi, Mother Therese of Calcutta, India with the extreme, grinding poverty that prevails there? What would he have thought of the Boer War, the two world wars, the Russian Revolution the systematic and orchestrated murder of twenty six million people by Hitler and Stalin in their mad quest for power, notwithstanding the millions who gave their lives in the two world wars to subdue the German war machine? Northern Ireland, the Middle East Conflicts, Vietnam, Bosnia, Herzegovina,

Rwanda and Burundi, Somalia, Zambia, Mozambique, Angola, Zimbabwe the Congo and Southern Africa. Robert Mugabe World Wide Web, World Wide Terror, Bin Laden, Religious Intolerance, young people being encouraged to achieve martyrdom by strapping high explosives to themselves in order to blow up and kill as many people as possible, HIV Aids, and the prospect of "making a man with blonde hair and a tan" not that far off. Would he even comprehend it? It's all too much!!

And as mankind continues to squabble, the superpowers flexing their nuclear capability muscles, we continue to live in a world that gets more unstable and violent by the day. It seems as if nowhere is safe any longer, life has no value and it would seem we are moving back to the principle of the survival of the fittest. Have we not learned anything in the last 2000 years except how to kill each other more efficiently? Will mankind ever step back and stop all of the madness and conflict that is the history of our world. Modern business that is considered "legitimate" is tinged with sordid behaviour and shady dealing, and the banks grow more powerful by the day. People are got rid of from secure jobs usually just before retirement to save the company money in pension settlements. Pension Funds are plundered and go bankrupt leaving thousands of loyal retirees at the mercy of social support. Grasping greed is, I believe destroying humanity while executives pat each other on the back in celebration of their ruthlessness. The political front is no better with world leaders loosing credibility with every new broadcast of their half truths and suspect policy.

And so the question is; WHERE WILL WE BE IN ANOTHER TWO HUNDRED YEARS, AND WHAT HORROR'S AWAIT OUR OFF SPRING????

And yet after having lived fifty-five years in this world, we are gotten old just the same, and what have we done, what have we done more than we did two hundred years ago in the old humdrum way?

Reitz's verse to his sons after the Boer War and self-imposed exile to Madagascar in 1903.

South Africa
Whatever foreign shores my feet must tread,
My hopes for thee are not yet dead.
Thy freedom's sun may for a while be set,
But not forever, God does not forget.